PUMPKIN
PLANS

For Cliff. Thank you for all your support and kindness throughout my career. Stay strong and keep smiling

:) *xxx*

EGMONT

We bring stories to life

First published in Great Britain in 2019
by Egmont UK Limited
The Yellow Building, 1 Nicholas Road, London W11 4AN

ISBN 978 1 4052 9392 1

A CIP catalogue record for this title is available from the British Library

68978/001

Printed and bound in Great Britain by CPI Group

AMELIA FANG
and the
LOST YETI TREASURES
LAURA ELLEN ANDERSON

EGMONT

CONTENTS

THE YETI MOUNTAIN PITS
AND THE ANCIENT YETI RESIDENTS
MAIN ENTRANCE PIT
MAIN TUNNEL
TEA PIT
ROYAL GUEST PIT FOR TANGINE
PHILLIS PODWICK
MARGOT FABWICK
ART PIT
HAROLD AND BETTY BUDWICK
JANE KNICKERWICK
JAMIE AND LILLITH LITTERWICK
TOILET
MAIN TUNNEL
MOUNTAIN STAIRCASE
SCOOBS LABRAWICK
TONAL TUFFWICK
ALILOOLA DOUGLEWICK
HELENA BOYLESWICK
TOILET
THE PRANCING PRACTICE PIT
GEORGIO BIGWICK
SALLY HAMMERWICK
SIOBHAN MCDERMOWICK
SARAHAHA LEVISWICK
AMY KITCHERWICK
SINGING PIT
RAINER-LEMON STOYERSWICK
PEACE AND QUIET PIT
ARM PIT
STEPH MUGGUMSWICK
SHOUTING PIT
JESSICA HARTWICK
EMMELON AND ANDY JOLLYWICK
CREATIVITY PIT
PAMPER PIT
GLADYS CANDLEWICK
TOILET
YETI LAUNDRY PIT

GUEST PIT
THE YETI GARDENS
CAKE PIT
THE PARTY PIT
MAIN TUNNEL
TEA PIT
TOILET
STAN STANWICK
BILL BUMWICK
SILLY PIT
CLEMENCE SPUDWICK
TOILET
DEREK BODWICK
GAVIN THE GRUFF GROTWICK
KENNETH AND MOLLY SPITWICK
KARLOS AND ZOEL NEWSON-WICK
ALLISON MCDIVIWICK
WICKY-WICK WICKWICK
GARY NORTHWICK
CASPAR HUBBLEWICK
ALEXIS AND LORNAPALOOZA KILLIWICK
GILLIAN AND MATTICUS TIMMWICK
TOILET
ROSANNA TALESWICK
YETI SHOWER PIT
SAMMIE AND STEVIE WOODAWICK
MAIN TUNNEL
TEA PIT
BERTY AND BENJI BOTTOMWICK
STINKY PIT
JANET NICEWICK
CHLOE AND PEDRO DUGWICK
SHEILA FLOWICK
INGRID AND SHAUN ANDERSWICK
MARIE ANDERSWICK
THE COOKING PIT
THE EATING AND DRINKING PIT
YETI RUBBISH PIT

Ghoulish Greetings!
AMELIA FANG
LIKES:
The Pumpkineers Club
Making new friends
DISLIKES:
Arguments with friends
Missing out on pumpkin activities
TANGINE
LIKES:
'EveryKing Sparkles' polish
Being fabulous
DISLIKES:
A messy room
Lack of beauty sleep
FLORENCE
LIKES:
Digging pits
Prancing
DISLIKES:
Being far away from friends
Being grumpy
GRIMALDI
LIKES:
Helping his friends
Snacking on pickled eyeballs
DISLIKES:
Any form of slide
Being alone

CLEMENCE
LIKES:
Vintage super-belch
All things pumpkin!
DISLIKES:
A dull party
Not enough glitter
LAURENCE
LIKES:
Looking after ancient yetis
His daughter Florence
DISLIKES:
A yeti in danger
Being woken up too early
SQUASHY
LIKES:
Tummy tickles
Hugs
DISLIKES:
Amelia and her friends disagreeing
Bringing up seed balls
LIKES:
Wearing sparkly tiara
Showing off sparkly tiara
DISLIKES:
Not wearing sparkly tiara
Losing sparkly tiara
MARGOT

I AM NOT A BEAST

CHAPTER 1

UNICORN FART AND MAGNIFICENCE

'BIIIIIIIIIIIRFNIIIIGHT BUMS!'

Amelia Fang woke with a start. Her pet pumpkin, Squashy, rolled off the bed, landing with a pa-doing!

'It can't be night time already, surely?!' said Amelia, pulling the blanket over her head.

'SOUNDS LIKE THE CELEBRATIONS 'AVE STARTED,' said Florence Spudwick with a stretch.

Grimaldi Reaperton yelped and hid underneath his bed covers.

It was the Winter Holidays in the Kingdom of the Dark, which meant six whole weeks off school! Young vampire Amelia Fang and her three best friends were spending the first weekend of their holidays at the Yeti Mountain Pits. The pits were home to all the ancient retired yetis in the kingdom, each living in their own cosy pit connected by a network of candlelit tunnels.

Florence's Grand-yeti Clemence was turning three hundred and fifty years old, and the ancient yetis were having a party all weekend to celebrate. Amelia and her friends were so excited to have a big sleepover together. This meant late-day chats, tragic stories by candlelight and lots of silliness.

The door to the pit where Amelia, Florence and Grimaldi were staying burst open. An old yeti bellowed, 'TIME FOR BIRFNIGHT BUMS!'

before running away.

'Florence, why does everyone keep shouting "Birthnight Bums"?' squeaked Grimaldi from under the covers. The little grim reaper was easily alarmed.

'BUMPING BUMS IS A COMMON YETI GREETING, LIKE SHAKING HANDS,' said Florence, as she lit the candles on the walls of the pit. 'IT'S TRADITION TO BUMP BOTTOMS WITH THE BIRFDAY YETI THE SAME NUMBER OF TIMES AS THEIR AGE.'

'Wait! Isn't your grand-yeti three hundred and fifty years old?' said Amelia. 'That means . . .'

'YUP! FREE 'UNDRED AND FIFTY BUM BUMPS,' said Florence. She performed five intense squats and punched the air. 'I'M SO READY FOR THIS!'

Florence Spudwick was a rare breed of yeti with a passion for one-armed press ups and having fun with her friends.

'AND I CAN'T WAIT FOR YOU TO MEET MY GRAND-YETI CLEMENCE,' she said happily. 'I FINK YOU'LL LOVE 'ER!'

The door to the pit flew open again, making Squashy do a tiny poo in shock. A HUGE yeti with curly white hair and thick-rimmed glasses ducked into the room.

'ALWITE DAD!' Florence grinned and the two yetis high-fived each other.

'EVENIN' FLO! ALWITE KIDS?' said Florence's dad, Laurence Spudwick. 'I 'OPE YOU ALL SLEPT WELL. WE GOT A LOT OF CELEBRATING TO DO OVER THE NEXT TWO NIGHTS!'

'Evening, Mr Spudwick!' said Amelia politely. 'We all slept as soundly as dead toads! These pits are super comfy.'

'THAT'S FANGTASTIC TO 'EAR!' replied Laurence. 'Y'KNOW, THE ANCIENT YETIS

WILL BE SO DELIGHTED TO MEET FLO'S FRIENDS. DON'T WORRY THOUGH, THEY DON'T ALL SPEAK LIKE US. ONLY RARE BREEDS 'AVE SUCH BEAUTIFUL BOOMING VOICES.' Laurence looked proud and grinned. 'YOU'RE PROB'LY RELIEVED THOUGH. IMAGINE SPENDING AN 'OLE WEEKEND SURROUNDED BY SHOUTING?!'

'I did wonder,' said Grimaldi thoughtfully.

'So, how many pits are there inside Yeti Mountain?' asked Amelia curiously.

'THERE ARE LOADS,' said Florence. 'DAD DUG THE 'OLE LOT WHEN 'E WAS STILL AT DIGGER SCHOOL!

'E COMES 'ERE EVERY NIGHT TO LOOK AFTER ALL THE ANCIENT YETIS. AND WHEN I'M GROWN UP I WANNA DO THE SAME.'

'THAT'S MY GIRL!' said Laurence, giving his daughter a big sloppy kiss on the head.

'DAAAAAAAD, *GROSS!*' moaned Florence, wiping the slobber from her fur.

'RIGHT, I BEST GO GET BREKKY SERVED,' said Laurence, rubbing his paws together. 'WE GOT SUPER SLIMY SLOW WORMS WITH TONGUE-FLUFF SPREAD. GO GET YERSELVES SOME BEFORE DEREK EATS THE LOT. 'E LOVES 'IS TONGUE-FLUFF!' And Laurence stomped out of the room.

Suddenly, from the pit opposite, Prince Tangine La Floofle the First emerged. His hair was extra glittery, his fangs were sparkling white and his face was positively glowing.

'ARGH!' Florence bellowed, covering her eyes. 'DON'T LOOK DIRECTLY AT IT.'

Tangine scowled. 'How dare you,' he said before stroking both cheeks. 'I've never felt better. I discovered this new all-purpose glitter polish in my monthly *Pampered Prince* magazine. It's called EveryKing Sparkles. You really can use it on EVERYTHING – nails, cheeks, hair, fangs and SHOES.'

He waved his foot around, causing flecks of light to bounce off the walls. 'The results are phenomenal!'

Amelia squinted. 'More like *fluorescent.'*

'I'm kind of glad you're sleeping in your own room this weekend,' said Grimaldi, using the hood of his black robe to shield his eyes.

Florence's dad had insisted that Prince Tangine – half-vampire, half-fairy – have his very own pit for the duration of his stay.

Florence had tried telling her dad that Tangine didn't need any special 'royal' treatment, but Tangine had lapped up the attention. 'More room for my weekend stash of EveryKing Sparkles polish!' he had declared cheerfully.

'Can anyone else smell . . . unicorn fart?' asked Amelia.

'AND MAGNIFICENCE?' Florence added. 'Y'KNOW THAT KINDA SOUR, SWEET, SICKLY SMELL. A BIT LIKE GLORY, BUT MORE SYRUP-Y.'

'That'll be the polish!' Tangine confirmed. Squashy sniffed at Tangine's shoes and began to lick them.

'It's polish, Squashy,' said Tangine, 'not food.'

'Where's Pumpy this weekend?' asked Grimaldi.

'Grounded,' said Tangine, straightening his bow tie. 'He's been a very naughty pumpkin,

so Mum is getting a pumpkin trainer in over the Winter Holidays!'

Pumpy was Tangine's pet pumpkin, and a bit of a handful at times. But Tangine still loved him very much.

'Now, let's get to this party!' said Tangine, throwing a silky scarf around his neck.

Amelia and her friends made their way along the candlelit tunnels to the Party Pit dressed in extra-warm layers. The Yeti Mountain pits were incredibly cold; colder than anywhere Amelia had been before. She had learnt from her *Positively Pumpkin* magazine that pumpkins did NOT like the cold and liked to find cosy spaces to keep warm.

(Amelia loved everything to do with pumpkins and wanted to be a pumpkinologist when she grew up!) So, in order to keep Squashy snug, she had knitted him a spotty onesie for the weekend.

The friends entered the Party Pit, which was decorated from top to bottom with bunting, cobwebs and pictures of Florence's Grand-yeti Clemence. In the middle of the room sat a round table with the largest spread of frightful food Amelia had ever seen – it was even more impressive than the petrifying platter at her mother's annual Barbaric Ball! Vessels of bubbly green liquid fizzed and gurgled, assorted scabs sat in bowls beside toe-jam pastries, and splattered spleen oozed out from between layers of spider-leg sponge cake. It all looked disgustingly delicious!

Tangine gasped. '*That* is one of the best things I have EVER seen . . .'

'I KNOW!' agreed Florence enthusiastically. 'FIRST OF ALL I'M GONNA START MAKING A DENT IN THE SPIDER-LEG SPONGE, THEN THOSE SCABS ARE ALL MINE AND THEN –'

'No, not the food,' Tangine replied, shaking his head dreamily. 'That . . . *right there* . . . is the *best thing* I've ever seen!' He skipped over to a baffled-looking yeti and stroked the sparkly tiara on her head. 'It's GLORIOUS,' he breathed.

'Oh!' The yeti blushed. 'It's me favourite fing ever, this is! I wear it ALL the time.' But Tangine, like a jittery magpie, had already danced over to a picture of Grand-yeti Clemence that stood on the table between the bowls of assorted scabs.

'Actually, these glittery glasses may top the tiara,' he squealed. 'I must ask Florence's Grand-yeti where they're from!'

'THEY'RE FROM *THE GLITTEROPOLIS EYEDOLS,'* said the picture of Grand-yeti Clemence, making Tangine almost jump right out of his skin. 'HEE HEE! THAT TRICK NEVVA GETS OLD!' The old yeti chortled as she removed the picture frame from her face.

'YOU MUST BE ONE OF FLO FLO'S FRIENDS!' said Grand-yeti Clemence as she crawled out from underneath the table. 'YOU SMELL OF UNICORN

FART AND MAGNIFICENCE. I LIKE YOU ALREADY.'

'I'm Prince Tangine La Floofle the FIRST,' said Tangine proudly. 'Friend of Florence and future king of Nocturnia.'

Grand-yeti Clemence bellowed with laughter. 'YOUR NAME IS RIDICULOUSLY LONG AND ALSO SOUNDS LIKE FOOD. SO I'M JUST GONNA CALL YOU DAVE. NICE TO MEET YOU, PRINCE DAVE.'

350

CHAPTER 2

DRAW ME LIKE ONE OF YOUR YETIS

''APPIEST OF BIRFNIGHTS, GRAND-YETI!' Florence boomed. She pranced over to her Grand-yeti Clemence as if she were as light as a feather. The two yetis turned back to back and bumped their bottoms together over and over and over again . . . until three hundred and fifty bum bumps later, Grand-yeti Clemence pulled Florence into a big fluffy hug.

'OH FLO FLO!' she laughed. 'YOU'RE TALLER AND WIDER EVERY TIME I SEE YOU.

YOU ARE SUCH A BOLD BEAUTY!'

Clemence may have been three hundred and fifty years old, but she certainly had BUNDLES of energy, and oodles of *style*. She was dressed in a pair of colourful baggy trousers and a flowing top and had glittery jewels of all shapes and sizes intertwined in the long braids that covered her head.

'YOU'VE ALREADY MET TANGINE . . . I MEAN, DAVE!' said Florence, winking at her grand-yeti.

Tangine rolled his eyes.

'THESE ARE MY UVVA BEST FRIENDS, AMELIA AND GRIMALDI,' said Florence.

'Happy Birthnight, Clemence!' said Amelia, giving a little curtsey. Grimaldi waved nervously.

'OOH!' Grand-yeti Clemence gasped. She seemed very excited about Squashy, who was bouncing around Amelia's ankles.

'IS THAT A *PUMPKIN?*'

'This is my pet pumpkin, Squashy,' said Amelia. 'Would you like to hold him?'

Clemence gasped. 'OH, YES PLEASE!'

'WELL, I'M GONNA GO PRANCE WHILST YOU GUYS TALK ALL FINGS PUMPKIN!' said Florence, before grabbing Tangine's hand. 'AND YOU'RE GONNA BE MY PRANCE PARTNER.'

'Wait, I must stretch my fabulous limbs first . . .' Tangine proclaimed, but he barely had a chance to finish his sentence because Florence was already dragging him on to the dance floor.

Amelia scooped Squashy up and handed him over to Grand-yeti Clemence. The old yeti giggled and hugged Squashy. 'OH, YOU ARE ADORABLE! I *LOVE* PUMPKINS!'

'So do I!' said Amelia happily. 'I love them so much I've joined a new pumpkin club called the Pumpkineers. It's so much fun – we learn loads of pumpkin facts and I've met lots of other creatures who love pumpkins ALMOST as much me.'

'Nobody could love pumpkins as much as you, Amelia,' said Grimaldi with a grin. 'Don't you have a big pumpkin patch party coming up soon?'

'It's tomorrow actually,' said Amelia. 'I keep forgetting to tell Florence that I won't be able to stay here for the whole weekend. I'd already said yes to Clemence's birthday party before I got my invitation to the pumpkin patch party. But I figured I could do both. One night for each!'

'Wow, two parties in one weekend!' said Grimaldi. 'You're one wild vampire!'

The two friends giggled.

'I'd better go and tell Florence now before I forget again,' said Amelia.

'TELL ME WHAT?' said Florence, making Amelia jump. She had pranced back over without so much as a sound.

'Oh, hi Florence!' Amelia stammered. 'I actually meant to tell you sooner, but I thought I might be able to party here for a bit and then go to the —'

But she was interrupted by a yeti shouting 'PREEEEEEEEESENTS!' at the top of their voice.

‘WOOHOOOOOOO!’ shrieked Grand-yeti Clemence, as a startled Squashy jumped out of her arms and back into Amelia’s. ‘COME ON KIDS. ’ELP ME OPEN MY PILE OF TREATS!’ Then she was ushered by the excitable yetis over to a huge stack of gifts.

After unwrapping a scream-tea maker, a snot-collector and at least three toenail hats, Florence gave Grand-yeti Clemence her birthday gift.

‘I FINK YOU’LL LIKE THIS, GRAND-YETI,’ said Florence, handing over a small box she’d wrapped in spotty paper.

Clemence smiled and carefully unwrapped her present. When she opened the glittery box and saw the necklace inside, she gasped, putting a paw to her mouth.

‘Wait a minute,’ said Tangine, marching forward to admire the gem. ‘That’s a pure Glitteropolis Garnet! I’ve never seen one up close before. It’s so beautiful!’

‘IT’S . . . IT’S . . .’ stammered Grand-yeti Clemence before throwing her arms around Florence in delight. ‘OH, FLO FLO!’

‘DOES THIS MEAN YOU LIKE IT?’ Florence asked earnestly.

Grand-yeti Clemence held the necklace up to the candlelight so that the glittery gem made the whole room sparkle. ‘I ABSOLUTELY *LOVE* IT, FLO FLO,’ she said,

staring at the jewel in awe. 'THIS MUST'VE BEEN SO EXPENSIVE. I 'OPE YOU DIDN'T SPEND *ALL Y*OUR MOON COINS ON ME?!'

Florence shrugged. 'I'LL SAVE 'EM UP AGAIN,' she said. 'YOU ONLY TURN FREE 'UNDRED AND FIFTY ONCE, EH!'

Clemence put the necklace on and twirled around. 'DON'T I LOOK RAVISHING?!' she said happily. 'I FINK THIS CALLS FOR SOME VINTAGE SUPER-BELCH.' The old yeti handed out cups of the bubbling green liquid to Amelia and her friends.

Amelia took a sip and immediately began to float a few inches off the ground. 'Wow! This is some strong belch!' she said before burping loudly and gently landing back on the ground.

Florence took a sip and did a floaty somersault in the air. 'THIS IS THE BEST BELCH I'VE EVVA TASTED!'

Grimaldi drank his whole cup and ended up

stuck on the ceiling, looking a little worse for wear.

'Wow!' he said through wide eyes. 'What's IN that belch?'

'MY FATHER, TERRENCE SPUDWICK, MADE IT AGES AGO WHEN 'E USED TO LIVE IN THESE PITS TOO. THIS 'ERE IS THE FINEST, MOST BELCHIEST SUPER-BELCH YOU'LL EVVA DRINK,' chuckled Clemence.

'I'll say!' said Amelia, gazing up at Grimaldi.

'SADLY, THESE ARE THE ONLY BOTTLES LEFT,' said Clemence, pointing to the small stash on the table.

'CAN'T YOU MAKE MORE?' said Florence.

'IT'S A TOP SECRET RECIPE. ME DAD DIDN'T TELL ANYONE – NOT EVEN ME!' said Clemence. 'SO, WHEN 'E PASSED, THE RECIPE WENT WIV 'IM. THE CHEEKY WOTSIT.'

'Well, that makes it EXTRA special!'

said Amelia before taking another sip and feeling herself rise upwards, bottom-first.

'EXACTLY!' said Clemence, then she turned to Tangine. 'I BELIEVE YOU'RE STAYING IN TERRENCE'S OLD ROOM! NOW *THAT'S* AN HONOUR,' she said.

'Ah! I wondered who the old yeti in all the pictures was!' said Tangine. 'Well, he can sure make a great brew!' He raised his cup of belch with a grin.

'I DO MISS 'IM LOADS!' said Clemence. 'BUT AT LEAST 'E LIVES ON THROUGH 'IS SUPER-BELCH, AND WHAT BETTER WAY TO APPRECIATE IT THAN WIV FAMILY AND FRIENDS, EH?' She gulped her cup of super-belch down in one and float-cartwheeled into the centre of the room. 'COME ON KIDS, LET'S DO SOME FLOATY PRANCING!'

By midnight, the birthnight celebrations were in full swing. There were entertainers from all over the kingdoms, including a leprechaun jig teacher called Mr McMarvellous, a toad top-hat maker called Sir Ribbit and a famous uni-angel-bunny artist, Clifford Harris.

'YOU WON'T FIND ANYONE IN ALL THE KINGDOMS AS GOOD AT PAINTING YETIS AS CLIFFORD,' said Florence's dad. 'E'S WELL KNOWN FOR 'IS BRILLIANT USE OF GLITTER PAINTS. CLEMENCE WAS SO 'APPY WE COULD BOOK 'IM IN!'

'I use only the *finest* glitter paints mixed

with the freshest fire tears of the most majestic Flamingo-dragons,' pronounced Clifford. He stroked his glittery beard in deep thought, then prepared a new blank canvas. 'Who is my first subject?' he asked.

Tangine, who had been stuffing his face with pickled eyeballs, shouted, 'ME!' He marched across the room, spreading himself out on the chaise-longue in front of Clifford's easel, before placing a hand on his forehead.

'Draw me like one of your yetis,' he said airily.

Whilst Tangine had his portrait done,

Amelia and Grimaldi were digging into the delightfully disgusting feast.

'Galloping goblins,' said Amelia. 'I still haven't told Florence about the pumpkin patch party!'

'Best do it now,' said Grimaldi, looking a little worried. 'Just in case she starts making plans for us tomorrow.'

'I'll do it, don't worry,' said Amelia, swallowing a pickled eyeball. 'I'm having such fun, I wish I didn't have to leave early. But I really want to go to the pumpkin patch party too. I'm sure Florence will understand.'

CHAPTER 3

EMBRACE YOUR INNER YETI

'UNDERSTAND WHAT?' said Florence, making Amelia jump again.

'Bothering batwings, Florence,' gasped Amelia. 'You keep making me jump with your soundless prancing!'

Florence puffed out her chest proudly. 'TOP NOTCH PRANCER, ME! SO, WHAT'S UP?'

'Well, you know that it's the Pumpkineers' pumpkin patch party tomorrow?' said Amelia.

'OH, IS IT?' said Florence, before gulping down a mug full of super-belch and floating towards the ceiling bum-first.

'Well, I'd really like to go along since it's

a special party to welcome all the new Pumpkineers,' called Amelia. 'So would it be okay if I asked your dad to call my mum so she can pick me up a bit –'

'WHAT?!' said Florence. 'I CAN'T 'EAR YOU FROM UP 'ERE . . . SPEAK UP!'

Amelia raised her voice. 'I need to leave a night –'

'BUUUUUUUUUUUURRRRRRRP,'

Florence bellowed, before slowly floating back down to ground level. 'SORRY 'BOUT THAT . . . I FORGOT 'OW STRONG THAT SUPER-BELCH IS! OKAY, WHAT WERE YOU SAYING?'

Amelia tried again.

'So, at moonrise tomorrow, I need to lea—'

But before she could finish, a horde of ancient yetis gathered around the food table and began singing loudly.

'HAPPY BIRTHNIGHT TO YOUUUUU
FULL OF GLITTER AND GOOOOOO
WE HOPE IT'S A NIGHTMARE
WITH MANY LUMPS IN YOUR STEEEEW!'

Florence's dad brought in a HUGE mud-worm cake, decorated with three hundred and fifty lit candles. It looked as though the whole thing was on fire.

'Make a wish! Make a wish!' said a small stout yeti, before marching right up to Grand-yeti Clemence and yelling, '**MAKE IT!**' in her face.

Clemence sucked in a huge breath, then blew with all her might. A few yetis had to duck as the candle flames went soaring across the room. Everyone cheered, coughed and spluttered as Grand-yeti Clemence closed her eyes tight and made her wish.

The mud-worm cake was shared out amongst the yetis, then Florence drank another mouthful of super-belch, and floated above the crowd. She cleared her throat to get their attention, then said proudly.

'I JUST WANNA SAY A BIG 'APPY BIRTHNIGHT TO MY GRAND-YETI CLEMENCE. 'ERE'S TO ANUVVA FREE 'UNDRED AND FIFTY YEARS!'

Everyone raised their arms, then

bum-bumped each other and made a toast, 'TOOOOOO CLEMENCE!'

Florence continued. 'AND I'M SO 'APPY TO BE ABLE TO SPEND THIS 'OLE WEEKEND WIV MY MY BESTEST FRIENDS IN THE ENTIRE KINGDOMS.' She smiled at Amelia, Grimaldi and Tangine. 'FANKS FOR COMING 'ERE WIV ME. WE'RE GONNA 'AVE SO MUCH FUN!' Florence burped loudly, the yetis cheered, and she floated back down to ground level.

Uh oh, thought Amelia. She *really* needed to tell Florence about having to leave the party early!

But that was going to have to wait. A yeti grabbed Amelia's hand and before she knew it, she was being dragged on to the dance floor to perform a traditional yeti prance.

'EMBRACE YOUR INNER YETI!' Florence bellowed, joining the prancing chain of yetis.

It was a graceful dance, and the yetis moved around the room with barely a sound.

The best part was watching Tangine try to get the hang of it. He gradually became a tangle of limbs and wings before falling flat on to his bottom. 'All *I* want to embrace is an ice pack for my sore derrière,' he groaned.

After an intense game of musical statues, the yetis decided to play hide and seek. There were certainly PLENTY of places to hide in the Yeti Mountain.

'OKAY EVERYONE,' bellowed Clemence. 'I'M GONNA COME FIND YOU IN FIRTY SECONDS!' She sat on a sofa chair and covered her eyes with her paws. 'READY . . . STEADY . . . GO! FIRTY . . . TWENNY NINE . . . TWENNY EIGHT . . .'

The pits rumbled and shook as the ancient yetis thundered out of the Party Pit at some speed. Amelia, Florence, Grimaldi and Tangine ran into the tunnels, hearts pounding with adrenaline. Squashy excitedly bounced behind them with a pa-doing, pa-doing, pa-doing.

'WE NEED TO SPLIT UP,' said Florence. 'THE YETIVATOR WILL TAKE YOU TO DIFFERENT LEVELS IF YOU WANNA GET

FURVA AWAY! *GO, GO, GO!'* Then she ran off and disappeared around a corner.

'I'm going to hide in the toilets!' said Grimaldi, floating off towards the end of the tunnel. 'Nobody will expect that!'

'Eww,' said Tangine. 'So gross. I'm going to steal Clemence's idea and pretend I'm a portrait! She'll never suspect.' And he ran off back towards the Party Pit.

Amelia picked Squashy up and looked from side to side. 'Well, I guess we should hurry up and find a good hiding place,' she said as she headed towards the yetivator.

Amelia pressed a big red button on the wall and the doors to the yetivator slid open with a loud DING.

'MAIN LEVEL,' said a flat sort of voice.

Amelia stepped into the lift. She stared at the buttons on the wall and felt her brain do a roly-poly. It certainly wasn't as simple as just picking a floor. As well as numbered buttons, there were buttons with arrows pointing up, down, left, right and diagonally – not to mention buttons with all sorts of other symbols on them.

'Well, I'm going to have to press *something,'* Amelia said to Squashy. 'Otherwise Grand-yeti Clemence will find us straight away!'

From the Party Pit further down the corridor, Amelia heard Clemence shout, 'AND ONE! READY OR NOT, HERE I COME!'

Squashy squeaked in response.

'Okay, okay . . . here goes, Squashy!' said Amelia urgently. 'I've NO idea where this will take us, but hopefully we'll find a good hiding place!'

Amelia closed her eyes and poked at random buttons in no particular order. The doors to the yetivator closed.

'GOING UP, ROUND, BACK, OVER, DIAGONAL LEFT, UNDER AND UP ONCE MORE,' said the dull lift-voice.

'Uh oh,' said Amelia.

And the lift immediately began to move. Very, *very* quickly.

Amelia ended up pinned to the wall from the G-force of the lift shooting upwards. Squashy ricocheted off the walls as the yetivator swung around and did a loop-the-loop. It then began to move diagonally and around and around again, before whizzing upwards and eventually slowing to a stop.

The doors slid open with a DING.

Amelia stood still for a moment until her head stopped spinning. Squashy was quite green and coughed up a gooey seed ball. She picked him up carefully and stumbled out of the lift on very wobbly legs.

'Let's take the stairs next time,' said Amelia shakily, going to sit down on the floor. But as she did, something soft brushed past her leg, making her jump straight back up. 'GRIEVING GOBBLEPOTS!' she shrieked. But when Amelia looked down, nothing was there.

Amelia clutched Squashy to her chest.

Peering down the tunnel, over Squashy's green-tinged and slightly floppy stalk, she noticed a small bump underneath the carpet. It moved towards Amelia quickly and then, as if by magic, it simply disappeared.

CHAPTER 4

IT'S NOT BUMCHEEK POLISH!

'That was odd,' said Amelia, checking around her for signs of the mysterious bump.

Squashy sniffed at the carpet furiously. Then he began rolling along the corridor in the direction the strange bump had travelled.

'What's up, Squashy?' said Amelia, following him along the tunnel. He squeaked once, but then began to move so quickly that Amelia could hardly keep up. 'Squashy! Slow down, or I'll lose you!'

He sped around corners and **pa-doinged** up

a wonky staircase, stopping every so often to sniff the walls, before whizzing off again. After many twists and turns, clambering up countless stairs, and stumbling through tunnel after tunnel, Amelia found herself back where she'd started.

'Squashy!' she said, trying to catch her breath. 'I'm not sure if you've understood the rules of hide and seek? We're *meant to hide*!'

Finally Squashy came to a slow stop outside one of the yeti pits. He stared up at the door and frowned.

'What's wrong?' asked Amelia. 'Wait a

minute . . . this is Tangine's room. What's going on with you, Squashy? You're acting very strangely.'

Squashy *pa-doinged* once and squeaked in frustration. He nudged at the door which was slightly ajar, then rolled inside.

'Hey Squashy! You can't just roll into someone else's room! Come back!' Amelia hurried in after Squashy.

She gasped and stopped in her tracks. Tangine's pit was a complete mess.

It didn't make sense. Tangine was one of the tidiest creatures she knew. He even took great pride in organising his socks in order of softness. But there was certainly no order here. In fact, it looked as though Tangine had taken every one of his belongings and thrown them around the room in a complete frenzy. What *was* going on?

Squashy rolled underneath the bed and began squeaking loudly.

'Squashy! That's *enough*!' said Amelia sternly. As she reached under the bed, feeling along the wall to retrieve the little pumpkin, her hand got stuck in something slimy.

'EWWW!' she cried, pulling her hand away quickly. It was sparkling fiercely and smelt like unicorn fart and magnificence.

'This must be Tangine's special polish.' Amelia peered under the bed. Tangine's containers of EveryKing Sparkles were scattered on the floor, and they all seemed to be empty.

'What the bats has happened?!' said Amelia. 'Come on, Squashy, we'd better go and tell Tangine about this!'

'MY PRECIOUS POLISH!' Tangine bellowed when he saw the devastation in his pit.

'BOUNCING BATWINGS, TANGINE,' said Florence. 'WHAT YOU BEEN DOING?!'

'I didn't DO anything!' Tangine cried in despair, gathering up the empty polish containers. 'Look! There's not one bit left.'

'There's a tiny splodge on the floor there,' said Grimaldi, pointing to a corner of the pit, in an attempt to cheer Tangine up.

Tangine crawled over to the last remains of the glittery polish and scooped it up into the palm of his hand. 'I will never be the same

without you . . .' he whispered to the globule.

'Wow,' said Amelia, looking around the pit properly. 'Terrence really DID love his super-belch, didn't he?!'

The pit walls were covered from top to bottom with framed pictures of Terrence in various poses, nearly always holding a bottle of super-belch. Amelia giggled at one picture of Terrence cradling the belch like a baby.

''E SURE DID!' said Clemence's voice before the old yeti waltzed into Tangine's pit and chuckled. 'FOUND YOU! AND YOU AND YOU AND YOU!' she said, pointing at each of the friends in turn. 'AND . . . YOUUUUU!' She pointed at Squashy, who waggled his stalk merrily in response. 'YOU'RE NOT VERY GOOD AT THIS HIDE 'N' SEEK GAME.'

'That's because we STOPPED playing ages ago,' snapped Tangine.

'OI!' said Florence. 'DON'T TALK TO ME GRAND-YETI LIKE THAT.'

Tangine sighed. 'I'm sorry Clemence,' he said. 'Someone came into my pit and used ALL of my EveryKing Sparkles polish! My cheeks will never be shiny again.'

'OH, PRINCE DAVE, I'M TERRIBLY SORRY TO 'EAR THAT. ALTHOUGH I WOULDN'T WORRY TOO MUCH,' said Clemence. IT'S NOT LIKE ANYONE EVER SEES

YOUR CHEEKS ANYWAY.'

Tangine frowned in confusion.

'OH!' said Amelia, almost choking with laughter. 'It's not *bumcheek* polish!'

Clemence furrowed her fluffy eyebrows, then laughed out loud. 'AAAAH YOU MEANT THE UVVA CHEEKS, DIDN'T YOU!'

'Well, I'm glad you're finding this funny!' said Tangine miserably.

'OH, LIGHTEN UP YOU BIG TOE,' said Florence. 'I RECKON YOU JUST USED THE 'OLE LOT WIVOUT REALISING! IT WAS 'ARD TO LOOK DIRECTLY AT YOU.'

Tangine harrumphed, then raised his eyebrows. 'I suppose I COULD have . . .' he said thoughtfully. 'But *no*! I brought twenty tubs with me. Enough to last a whole weekend.'

'We're sorry, Tangine,' said Amelia, putting an arm around him. 'Come on, we'll help you tidy up this mysterious mess.'

'Who could've done this?' muttered Tangine, folding up pairs of socks into the tiniest neatest pile. 'Maybe someone is jealous of how fabulous I am!'

Amelia raised her eyebrows. 'I don't think *that's* the case,' she said. 'Plus, I didn't see anyone else when I was walking around.' She pondered for a second. 'Apart from a weird moving carpet lump.'

'"A weird moving carpet lump?"' echoed Tangine.

Amelia shrugged. 'I'm as baffled as you are,' she said.

'TANGINE, YOU BIN TRYIN' TO ESCAPE THROUGH THE WALL?' said Florence as she pulled out a pair of Tangine's glittery pantaloons and more socks from underneath the bed. 'THERE'S AN 'OLE THE SIZE OF SQUASHY UNDER 'ERE! BEST GET DAD TO PATCH THAT UP.'

'Are you kidding me?' said Tangine, folding his arms. 'Do I LOOK like I'd lie under the bed eating the WALL?!' His cheeks became flushed.

'CHILL OUT, YA BIG TOILET BRUSH,' said Florence, half-smiling. 'I WAS JUST MESSING WIV YA. PROB'LY JUST NEEDS SOME RE-DECORATING IN 'ERE.'

'SOME OF THESE PITS ARE AS OLD AS US ANCIENTS,' said Grand-yeti Clemence. 'I'M SURE A BIT OF PIT-FILLER WILL DO THE TRICK. LAURENCE'LL SORT IT OUT NO PROBLEM.' She put a hairy arm around a flustered Tangine. 'NOW, LET'S GO GET YOU A NICE CUP OF YET-TEA, THEN YOU CAN 'ELP ME FIND THE REST OF THE YETIS.'

'Well, I should imagine I *would* be the most fabulous person at finding everyone,' Tangine agreed grudgingly.

'QUITE RIGHT,' said Clemence, winking at the others and leading him away.

By the time Amelia, Florence and Grimaldi headed back to the Party Pit, Clemence and Tangine had managed to find all of the hidden yetis. The birthnight celebrations were back in full swing. A group of yetis created a yeti-pyramid, others were having a pus pie-gobbling competition and there was a huge queue to have glittery portraits painted by Clifford.

'I'M SO 'APPY YOU GUYS CAME TO CELEBRATE GRAND-YETI CLEMENCE'S BIRFNIGHT WIV ME!' said Florence. She pulled Amelia, Grimaldi and Tangine into a huge hug. 'EVEN IF IT'S ONLY FOR A SHORT TIME.'

'At least you had a whole night here before

you have to leave,' said Grimaldi to Amelia.

Florence loosened her grip and frowned.

'WHAT DO YOU MEAN *LEAVE*?' she asked.

'Oops,' said Grimaldi.

Amelia put a hand up to her mouth. 'Pottering pumpkins! I meant to tell you earlier. I've just been having so much fun, that I kept getting distracted and forgetting.'

Florence folded her arms.

'It's the Pumpkineers' pumpkin patch party tomorrow,' Amelia began. 'I was going to ask your dad to call my mum so she can collect me from here a night early, so I can go. I can't believe I have two parties in one weekend!'

Florence looked upset. 'YOU DON'T WANNA STAY 'ERE WIV US AND PLAY?'

Amelia was a little taken aback. 'Oh no! I mean, *yes*! Of course I do. If the pumpkin patch party hadn't fallen on the same weekend, I *definitely* would have stayed.

The Pumpkineers Club is brand new, so they're having a BIG party to welcome us all. It's going to be SO much fun and I've already met some other creatures who are *almost* as obsessed with pumpkins as I am!'

Florence grumbled and her frown deepened. 'SO, YOU'D RATHER HANG OUT WIV YOUR NEW FRIENDS THAN WIV US?'

'I didn't say that,' Amelia said, starting to feel a bit flustered. She really hadn't meant to upset Florence. 'Just because I have new friends doesn't mean I don't want to hang out with you guys.'

Florence looked down at the floor, avoiding eye contact with Amelia as everyone else shuffled awkwardly.

Squashy pa-doinged between Amelia and Florence, giving their feet reassuring nudges.

'Say something helpful,' whispered Tangine, poking an anxious Grimaldi.

Grimaldi picked up a tray from the food table. 'So . . . pickled eyeball anyone?'

CHAPTER 5

NOBODY LIKES CHANGE

Amelia slumped down on a chair and nibbled on a honey-roasted slow worm as she watched Florence on the dance floor with the ancient yetis.

‘Well, that went worse than I thought it would,’ said Grimaldi sadly.

‘I know,’ agreed Amelia. ‘I didn’t think Florence would get so upset about me leaving early.’

Grimaldi wasn’t very good at words, but he was good at listening and even better at hugs. He wrapped his arms around Amelia. ‘She’ll be okay,’ he said with a smile.

'Thanks Grimaldi,' said Amelia. 'I'm going to take a little walk outside. I think Squashy is due a poo break anyway . . .'

It was true. For the past half hour, Squashy had been producing some very unpleasant smells.

'I won't be long,' said Amelia.

'I'll just be here munching on eyeballs,' said Grimaldi.

The yeti gardens sat on a plateau at the very top of the Yeti Mountain. It was snowing heavily and long narrow icicles hung from the fluffy white petals of strange flowers.

Amelia wrapped her dad's velvet cloak around her shoulders tightly. It still smelt of Count Drake – a mixture of crossword puzzle paper and scream tea. It was comforting for Amelia, especially since she was feeling quite glum, confused and a bit cross. These were her least favourite feelings.

Whilst Squashy did his little pumpkin poos, she wandered around the ice-speckled gardens, before stumbling upon a large bare patch of snowy soil marked out by a small crooked wooden sign that read:

'CLEMENCE'S PUMPKINS –
DO NOT DISTURB.'

'STILL NUFFIN' GROWING . . .' said a voice, making Amelia jump. It was Clemence, holding a mug of vintage super-belch in one paw and a slice of mud-worm cake in the other.

'PLANTED A LOAD OF PUMPKIN SEEDS MONTHS AGO AND NUFFIN' EVER GREW,' said the old yeti, settling herself down next to the snowy soil of the pumpkin patch. 'ALL I EVVA WANTED WAS ME OWN

PUMPKIN PET! I EVEN WISHED FOR ONE TONIGHT WHEN I BLEW OUT ME CANDLES. YOU SAID YOU LOVED PUMPKINS, AMELIA. WHAT DO YOU FINK I'M DOING WRONG?'

Amelia let out a long sigh. She DID love pumpkins and would usually be super excited to talk about it. But it was pumpkins that had made Florence so upset with her!

'Um, it's pretty cold here in the mountains,' Amelia said quietly. 'That's why I knitted Squashy his onesie. Maybe it's too cold for your pumpkins to grow normally.' She scooped up Squashy who, having finished his business, was rolling round happily in the empty pumpkin patch.

Clemence tipped her big fluffy head to the side and looked at Amelia thoughtfully over the top of her spectacles. 'AH THAT'S A SHAME,' she replied. 'BUT FOR NOW. . . COME JOIN ME FOR A MINUTE.'

Clemence patted the ground next to her.

Amelia sat herself down next to the big old yeti and tried not to shiver too much. She didn't have the protection of wonderfully thick yeti fur and her bottom was very chilly on the snow.

'YOU AND FLORENCE 'AVE 'AD A DISAGREEMENT, 'AVEN'T YOU,' said Clemence. It wasn't really a question.

Amelia was shocked. 'I . . . We . . .' she stammered. 'We haven't really . . .'

Clemence put an arm around Amelia's shoulders. 'I'VE BEEN AROUND LONG ENUFF TO NOTICE THESE FINGS. ALSO, I 'EARD FLORENCE'S GRUMPY OUTBURST.'

Amelia looked at her feet and tickled Squashy's tummy for comfort.

'I feel bad, because I want to spend time with Florence and Grimaldi and Tangine,' said Amelia. 'But the Pumpkineers Club is really exciting too. There's a big pumpkin patch party tomorrow that I'd love to go to, but Florence got really upset about it.'

Amelia found the words pouring out of her mouth. She paused and frowned. 'I don't know why.'

Clemence smiled. 'HMMM. 'AVE YOU MADE NEW FRIENDS AT THIS PUMPKIN CLUB OF YOURS?' she asked.

Amelia nodded. 'All the Pumpkineers are SO nice, and we all love pumpkins, so we have *lots* to talk about.'

'THERE'S YOUR ANSWER THEN,' said Clemence. 'FLORENCE IS JUST A BIT JEALOUS.'

'Jealous of what?' said Amelia.

'OF YOU MAKIN' NEW FRIENDS,' said Clemence.

Amelia twiddled her thumbs. 'I . . . I didn't really think about that. Florence is one of my BEST friends and *always* will be. The Pumpkineers are just . . . well . . . *friends.*

They'll never be as special as Florence, Grimaldi and Tangine.' She looked up at Clemence. 'I feel bad now.'

'YOU SHOULDN'T FEEL BAD FOR MAKING NEW FRIENDS. IT'S PART OF LIFE!' said Clemence with a kind smile. 'AS YOU GROW UP, YOU'LL MEET LOTS OF NEW CREATURES. SO WILL FLORENCE. THAT'S WHAT MAKES LIFE EXCITING!'

Amelia looked up at Clemence. 'I guess we've always done *everything* together. But the Pumpkineers Club is just my thing. I want to be a pumpkinologist when I grow up and help poorly pumpkins.'

'FLORENCE WILL BE FINE!' said Clemence, giving Amelia a friendly squeeze. 'SHE'S NOT REALLY ANGRY WIV YOU. NOBODY LIKES CHANGE. BUT WHILST SOME FRIENDS WILL COME AND GO, WHAT YOU HAVE WITH FLORENCE, GRIMALDI AND TANGINE

IS SPECIAL. YOU'LL CARRY IT WIV YOU FOREVVA. FLORENCE WILL REALISE THAT SOON. AND ANYWAY, JUST WAIT 'TIL YOU GET OLD AND RETIRE LIKE ME. YOU WON'T BE ABLE TO GET RID OF YOUR FRIENDS! YOU'LL WISH YOU 'AD MORE FUN ACTIVITIES TO GET AWAY FROM 'EM!' She winked.

Amelia giggled.

'NOW, GO INSIDE AND GET PRANCING!' said Clemence, giving Amelia a nudge. 'I'M OFF FOR A YETI POWER NAP TO MAKE SURE I'M FULLY REFRESHED FOR THE FINAL PRANCE OF THE NIGHT!'

Amelia put both arms around Clemence and hugged her tight.

CHAPTER 6

JANE'S FLAMINGO-DRAGON KNICKERS

Amelia felt much more hopeful when she returned to the Party Pit. She decided to find Florence so that they could make up, but there was no sign of her on the dance floor in the mass of ancient yetis.

Grimaldi and Tangine, who were tango dancing (and surprisingly good at it), mentioned they'd last seen her at the food table gobbling a pus pie.

The party was starting to wind down now with lots of yetis already in bed. Amelia made up her mind to go and look for Florence in their room. But then she felt a tap on her shoulder. It was Margot, the yeti who usually wore a sparkly tiara.

'Um, excuse me,' Margot said politely. 'But have you seen my glittery tiara? I can't seem to find it anywhere.'

'I'm sorry, I haven't,' said Amelia. 'But I'll keep an eye out for it.'

The yeti looked sad. 'Thank you dear,' she said, and hobbled away to ask someone else.

'POOR MARGOT. THAT TIARA IS 'ER PRIDE AND JOY.'

Amelia turned in surprise to see Florence.

'I . . . 'ER . . . WELL, THE FING IS . . .' Florence stuttered, staring awkwardly at her paws.

Amelia's cold little vampire heart filled with hope when suddenly an almighty cry echoed through the tunnels.

Amelia and Florence turned to see what all the commotion was about. Derek the ancient yeti came trundling at full speed into the Party Pit and he did *not* look happy. In fact, he was frowning so hard that his fluffy eyebrows had completely covered his eyes.

'IT'S GONE!' he cried.

‘WHAT’S GONE, DEREK?’ asked Florence.

‘My bubble flute,’ Derek snapped, pointing his walking stick at Florence.

‘WHEN DID YOU LAST ’AVE IT?’ asked Florence.

‘I had it earlier on at the party,’ said Derek. ‘That flute is one of a kind: specially hand-carved by the oldest leprechaun in the Kingdom of the Light. It produces the glitteriest glitter bubbles you ever did see!’

‘DON’T WORRY, DEREK,’ said Florence. ‘I’LL ASK DAD TO PUT A PICTURE OF IT UP ON THE “MISSING FINGS” NOTICE BOARD ALONG WITH MARGOT’S TIARA . . .’

But before Florence could finish, Grand-yeti Clemence burst back into the Party Pit looking flustered.

‘FLO FLO!’ she cried.

‘WHAT’S GOING ON, GRAND-YETI?’ Florence said urgently.

'OH, FLO FLO!' said Grand-yeti Clemence in a wobbly voice. 'I WENT TO BED FOR MY POWER NAP WITH MY NECKLACE ON BECAUSE I NEVER WANTED TO TAKE IT OFF . . . THEN I SNEEZED AND WOKE MYSELF UP, AND NOTICED IT WAS GONE!'

'Are you sure it didn't fall off in your bed?' asked Amelia. 'Maybe we could have a proper look for you?'

'Or maybe you sneezed it right off?' said a sleepy Grimaldi.

'I'VE SEARCHED ALL OF MY BED, TOP, MIDDLE AND BOTTOM,' said Grand-yeti Clemence. 'I'VE SEARCHED MY 'OLE ROOM AND I CAN'T FIND IT ANYWHERE! I'M SO SORRY, FLO FLO. I FEEL AWFUL ABOUT IT.'

'IT'S NOT YOUR FAULT,' said Florence, giving her grand-yeti a hug. 'I'M SURE WE'LL FIND IT. WE CAN 'ELP YOU LOOK AT MOONRISE AFTER SOME SLEEP, YEH?'

Grand-yeti Clemence sniffed and nodded. Amelia and Florence guided Clemence back towards the yetivator at the end of the tunnel. Amelia felt ever so slightly sick at the memory of her last yetivator experience.

'DON'T WORRY, GRAND-YETI,' said Florence. 'WE'LL FIND IT. BEST GET SOME SLEEP BEFORE MORE CELEBRATIONS AT MOONRISE, EH!'

'YOU'RE RIGHT, FLO FLO.' Clemence kissed Florence on the forehead and pressed a big red button for the yetivator. 'YOU YOUNG ONES MAKE SURE YOU GET SOME SLEEP, TOO.'

As the yetivator doors opened, a yeti emerged, wearing a silky dressing gown.

'OH 'ELLO, JANE?' said Clemence. 'YOU LOOK SAD. WHAT'S WRONG?'

'Clemence, I'm so glad to see you,' she moaned. 'You won't believe this, but my favourite pair of glittery knickers have *gone*!'

'NOT THE ONES WITH THE FLAMINGO-DRAGONS ON THEM?' asked Clemence, stepping into the yetivator.

'Yes!' cried the yeti called Jane.

'OH, THEY WERE A LOVELY PAIR OF KNICKERS,' said Clemence, giving Jane a sympathetic rub on the back. 'I'VE LOST MY WONDERFUL NECKLACE, BUT I PROB'LY JUST SNEEZED IT OFF OR SUMFIN'.' Then she whispered, 'YOU 'AVEN'T GOT THE KNICKERS ON AND FORGOT 'AVE YOU?'

'Nope. I have my unicorn knickers on at the moment. Oh, I don't know how I'm going to live without my flamingo-dragon knickers,' sobbed Jane.

'Erm, I'm sure we could club together to buy you another pair?' Amelia suggested helpfully.

'Oh no.' Jane sniffed. 'They were LIMITED EDITION. The most glittery knickers there ever were and ever will be . . .'

Florence's dad came waltzing out of his pit in his pants. 'WHAT THE BATS IS GOING ON OUT 'ERE? WHY AREN'T YOU ALL IN BED?'

'GRAND-YETI'S NECKLACE 'AS GONE . . .'

Florence replied. 'AND SO 'AVE JANE'S FLAMINGO-DRAGON KNICKERS.'

'ALWITE, WELL, I'LL ADD 'EM TO THE "*MISSING FINGS*" NOTICE BOARD,' said Laurence. 'THOUGH IT SEEMS TO BE FILLING UP FAST.'

'Doesn't it seem a little odd that all these things have gone missing just after Tangine's pit got trashed? AND all of his glitter polish disappeared?' said Amelia. 'Not to mention that mysterious moving carpet bump I saw earlier.'

'MYSTERIOUS MOVING CARPET BUMP?' said Florence and her dad together.

'Did I not tell you?! I was so distracted by Tangine's messy room earlier, I must have forgotten,' said Amelia, her eyes wide. 'I saw it when we were playing hide and seek. Squashy followed it all the way back to Tangine's pit where we found the empty glitter polish tubs.' She paused for breath. '*Maybe* everything is connected in some way?'

Florence burst out laughing. 'I DOUBT IT!' she bellowed. ''OW CAN A MOVING CARPET BUMP MESS UP TANGINE'S ROOM AND TAKE ALL 'IS POLISH?!'

Laurence raised his eyebrows. 'WELL, THERE'S NUFFIN' WE CAN DO RIGHT NOW. IT'S VERY LATE AND WE'RE ALL VERY TIRED.' He yawned loudly. 'EVERYONE BACK TO YOUR BEDS, AND WE'LL SORT THIS OUT AT MOONRISE. I'M SURE THE MISSING FINGS WILL TURN UP. THEY'VE PROB'LY JUST GOT SWEPT UP WIV ALL THE CELEBRATIONS.'

Amelia, Squashy and Florence headed back to their pit and slumped into their beds. Grimaldi was already fast asleep, lightly snoring. Amelia hadn't realised how tired she was until she hit the pillow. Drifting off, she remembered that she and Florence hadn't really made up properly yet. Amelia sleepily raised her head to call to her friend when something in the shadows caught her eye. She squinted into the darkness, but nothing was there.

Amelia lay back down on to the pillow and fell into a land of dreams filled with pumpkin patches and fluffy white petals.

CHAPTER 7

I WOKE UP IN THE WALL

At midday, Amelia woke up so thirsty that even her fangs felt dry. She needed a glass of water.

Florence was snoring loudly, and Grimaldi was muttering in his sleep. Amelia thought he was perhaps dream-collecting dead toads. She wrapped her dad's cloak around her to keep warm and made sure not to wake Squashy as she slipped gently out of bed.

After having a drink in the kitchen pit, Amelia made her way back to bed. The tunnel was long and dimly lit and Amelia shivered despite the count's cloak. A candle went out ahead of her with a quiet hiss and then a long CREEEEEEEEEEEAK made Amelia almost jump out of her skin.

She swung round to see that it was just Tangine's pit door opening. 'Pottering pumpkins, Tangine, you made me jump!' she said, with a nervous laugh.

But nobody was there.

'Tangine?' Amelia whispered, leaning round the door into Tangine's pit. 'Tangine, where are you?'

There was no answer. Amelia frowned. *Perhaps he's gone to fetch a glass of water too?* she thought. But surely she would have seen him on her way back from the kitchen pit?

'Tangine?' Amelia called, holding her lantern up into the room to get a better look. And then she gasped.

Tangine's pit was an absolute MESS. Again.

'What the bats?' she whispered.

Amelia searched the pit high and low. She didn't spot a thing and Tangine was nowhere to be seen.

Amelia looked one last time, even checking under his bed, using the lantern to peer into the dark nooks and crannies. But there was still no sign of Tangine. Just a few scattered socks and the small hole in the wall.

She shuffled out from under the bed in frustration and bumped her head on one of the picture frames on the wall, causing it to fall off with a loud SMASH!

'*Grieving gobblepots!*' Amelia cried.

She picked up the broken frame, but as she did so, something fell out of the back.

Amelia watched as a very tatty piece of paper floated down to the ground. She picked it up and held her lantern close to get a better look. 'What *is* this?' she muttered.

Amelia could make out what looked to be some kind of map sketched on the paper with a large X at the very bottom. 'How odd,' she said.

Then she sighed – whatever it was didn't tell her where Tangine had gone or what had happened to his room. Tucking the mysterious map into her cloak pocket, she decided to sit outside Tangine's pit to wait for him to come back. She *had* to know he was okay before she went back to bed herself.

Amelia sat down, leaning against the wall with her dad's cloak pulled tightly around her. Minutes passed, and the harder she tried to stay awake, the more Amelia's eyelids began to droop. The last thing she remembered was seeing what looked like splodges of glitter all the way down the tunnel, before she fell into a deep slumber . . .

'Amelia . . .'

'Ameeeeelia?'

'AMELIA!'

Amelia awoke to find Tangine far too close to her face.

'Aaaaaagh!'

'Aaaaaaagh!' Tangine screamed back.

'Oh Tangine, you're back! Where *were* you?!' Amelia scrambled to her feet and hugged her friend.

'I woke up inside the wall,' Tangine said coldly.

'You what?' said Amelia, feeling confused.

'It was awful,' said Tangine grumpily. 'It took me forever to find my way back! I came out through that hole under my bed. Thank goodness I didn't come up through the toilet or something!'

'How the bats—' Amelia began, before loud yells echoing through the tunnels cut her off.

Florence and Grimaldi emerged from their pit into the tunnel.

'What's going on?' asked a sleepy and confused Grimaldi.

'THE MOON HAS ONLY JUST RISEN AND IT SOUNDS LIKE THE ANCIENT YETIS ARE ALREADY UP!' said Florence. 'THEY SURE KNOW 'OW TO PARTY. I FORT I WAS 'ARDCORE, BUT EVEN I CAN'T KEEP UP WIV 'EM.'

But as they headed towards the noise, the friends soon realised that the commotion was not celebratory at all.

A group of ancient

yetis were gathered around the notice board near the Mountain Pit entrance and they all looked very upset indeed.

'What's going on?' said Amelia, approaching the group of distressed yetis.

'S'CUSE ME, S'CUSE ME PLEASE,' said Florence as she made her way through the crowd.

The notice board was FULL to the brim with pictures of missing items.

A rare breed of yeti with glasses and slicked back hair was sticking a picture of a glittery ear scoop on to the board.

'BEST EAR SCOOP THERE EVVA WAS, Y'KNOW,' he said, wiping away a tear. 'IT ONCE SCOOPED AN 'OLE BROCCOLI OUTTA ME RIGHT EAR. NUFFIN' ELSE CLEANS ME EARS LIKE ME PRECIOUS EAR SCOOP.'

The yetis were becoming more agitated by the second. Amelia squeezed her way through the yetis, trying not to get wedged between them. They seemed to be arguing about whose missing shoe was the glitteriest.

'*MY* MISSING SHOE IS DEFINITELY MORE GLITTERY, THEREFORE IT'S MUCH MORE IMPORTANT!' said a curly-haired yeti.

'Don't be preposterous, Michelle,' said another yeti. '*MY* shoe is FAR glitterier. It almost BLINDED Derek when we went prancing last Wednesday.'

'SPEAKING OF BLINDED, ME GLASSES 'AVE GONE!' cried a yeti in a knitted jumper.

'Mine have gone too!' moaned someone else. 'EVERYTHING is blurry! I need my glasses!'

'AND MINE!'

'BEEEEEEEAST!'

Laurence bellowed suddenly.

A bunch of white-furred yetis, including Florence, suddenly threw their arms up in the air and all shouted at once:

'I AM NOT A BEAST, I'M A RARE BREED OF YETI!'

Then there was silence.

Florence's dad stepped forward. 'I FORT THAT MIGHT GRAB YOUR ATTENTION,' he said, putting his paws on his hips. 'I FINK WE NEED AN EMERGENCY PIT MEETING. EVERYONE IN THE PARTY PIT RIGHT NOW. WE GOT SOME ISSUES WE NEED TO ADDRESS!'

CHAPTER 8

GLITTERY AND FLOUNCY HORRORS

'IS EVERYONE 'ERE?' called Laurence.

The yetis muttered amongst themselves as the last few sat down. Clemence squeezed in next to Amelia, Florence, Grimaldi and a grumpy Tangine. Squashy was snoring quietly on Amelia's lap, clearly still tired from all the partying.

Laurence cleared his throat. The room fell silent.

'NOW WE'RE ALL 'ERE, PLEASE LISTEN CAREFULLY.' All eyes were on Florence's dad.

'AS SOME OF YOU MAY BE AWARE, THERE 'AVE BEEN REPORTS OF MISSING ITEMS THIS WEEKEND,' said Laurence, looking serious. 'AT FIRST, WE FORT THEY WERE JUST LOST. BUT NOW SO MANY FINGS ARE MYSTERIOUSLY DISAPPEARING, I BELIEVE THESE ITEMS *MAY* 'AVE BEEN . . . *STOLEN*.'

The room filled with shocked gasps, resulting in gasp-induced coughs and at least three cough-induced farts.

'NOW, THE MAIN THING IS NOT TO PANIC,' Laurence continued. 'BUT FIRST AND FOREMOST, I WILL NEED TO SEARCH EVERYONE'S PITS. I'M NOT SAYING ANY OF YOU ARE TO BLAME, BUT PERHAPS THERE'S BEEN A MIX-UP SOMEWHERE . . .'

'They're certainly not searching *my* pit,' said Tangine, folding his arms. 'No way.'

'I DON'T FINK YOU GET A CHOICE,' said Florence.

'But my room is a mess *AGAIN* and I don't know why. I haven't even had a chance to fold my collection of sparkly pants in rainbow order,' said Tangine.

'EVERYONE GO BACK TO YOUR PITS. I'LL BE SEARCHING EACH PIT IN TURN OVER THE NEXT FEW HOURS, SO PLEASE BE PATIENT WHILST I GET TO THE BOTTOM OF THIS MYSTERY!' Laurence announced.

The old yetis groaned and began to shuffle out of the party pit.

'GUESS THAT'S ME BIRFNIGHT CELEBRATIONS DONE THEN,' said Clemence sadly.

Back in their pit, Florence began doing extra fast 'stress-ups', Grimaldi sat hugging his scythe, and Amelia watched Squashy sniffing

around the walls. Tangine returned to his own pit to refold his sparkly pants in rainbow order and tidy up the mysterious mess (again). Everyone was very upset by this latest turn of events.

'What if Florence's dad doesn't find the missing things?' said Grimaldi. 'What if there is a thief around here? What if they think *I* stole them?!'

'DON'T BE SILLY,' said Florence. 'NOBODY WILL FINK THAT.'

In an attempt to distract everyone and lighten the mood, Amelia pulled out the strange map she'd found in Tangine's bedroom.

'Guys! Look what I found. It fell out from behind a picture in Tangine's room. I knocked it off the wall by accident after I looked under Tangine's bed. It's some kind of old map!'

'Ooo, there's an X on it. Maybe it's a treasure map!' said Grimaldi.

'DONT BE DAFT, GRIMALDI,' laughed Florence, studying the raggedy, glitter-stained map. 'ALTHOUGH WHAT I WANT TO KNOW, AMELIA, IS WHAT YOU WERE DOING UNDER TANGINE'S BED?! YOU NEVER KNOW WHAT GLITTERY AND FLOUNCY HORRORS YOU MIGHT FIND UNDER THERE.'

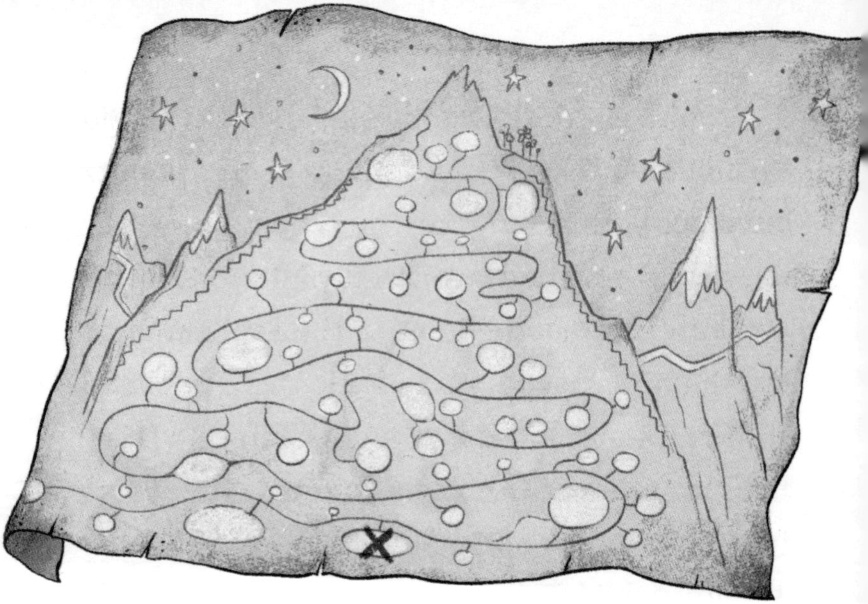

Amelia giggled and smiled at Florence, feeling relieved that things seemed much better between them after yesternight's argument.

'IT MIGHT NOT SHOW HIDDEN TREASURE BUT I FINK THAT'S AN OLD MAP OF THE PITS!' said Florence. 'WE SHOULD COME BACK TO THE YETI MOUNTAIN NEXT WEEKEND AND SEE WHERE IT LEADS! IT CAN BE LIKE A SECRET MISSION!'

'Oooh, I'd definitely be up for that,' said Grimaldi. 'As long as there's no danger involved.'

Amelia shuffled awkwardly. 'Well, I can't actually,' she said. 'Some of the Pumpkineers are having a petrifying picnic next weekend and I already said I'd go with them.'

'OH,' Florence grunted.

'Hey, and isn't it the pumpkin patch party tonight?' said Grimaldi.

'Oh, yeah,' said Amelia quietly, wishing Grimaldi would stop speaking. It was starting to look like she'd jumped the gun about things being better . . . She looked at Florence, but the yeti was staring at the floor. 'Um, Florence? Do you mind if I ask your dad to call my mum so she can come and pick me up?'

Florence frowned. 'MY DAD SAID WE 'AVE TO STAY IN OUR PITS SO 'E CAN INVESTIGATE THE DISAPPEARING ITEMS.'

'But I need to ask him now, otherwise I won't get to the pumpkin patch party in time,' said Amelia. 'I'm sure your dad won't mind, will he?'

'LOOK, I KNOW YOU'D RATHER GO BACK AND HANG OUT WIV YOUR NEW PUMPKIN MATES THAN STAY 'ERE,' said Florence looking sad. 'BUT DAD TOLD US TO STAY PUT.'

'That's not true, Florence,' said Amelia, feeling a bit shocked. 'And that's not a very nice thing to say.'

'WELL, 'OW AM I MEANT TO COMPETE WIV YOUR NEW FRIENDS WHO LOVE

PUMPKINS AS MUCH AS YOU?' said Florence.

'*Almost* as much . . .' Grimaldi corrected her. Florence and Amelia both frowned at him.

'I'm just saying!' squeaked Grimaldi.

'It's not a competition, Florence,' said Amelia. 'You don't have to be jealous.'

'JEALOUS?!' bellowed Florence. 'I'M NOT JEALOUS! YOU'RE THE ONE DITCHING US FOR YOUR NEW FRIENDS!'

'I'm not ditching anyone!' Amelia said hotly. She felt her cheeks flush and suddenly she lost her temper.

'But if you're going to be so grumpy about it, then maybe I WOULD rather hang out with my *new friends*!'

Florence looked shocked. Amelia *felt* shocked. Grimaldi gulped.

'Florence . . . I didn't mean . . .' Amelia started, but Florence interrupted.

'FINE,' she said coldly. 'I'LL ASK DAD TO CALL YOUR MUM RIGHT NOW.'

But as Florence reached for the door handle, the pit door burst open. Florence's dad was on the other side, looking flustered, and he was holding a sparkly tiara.

'Isn't that Margot's tiara? The one that went missing?!' gasped Amelia.

'IT IS,' said Laurence.

'WHERE WAS IT?' asked Florence.

'THAT'S THE FING . . .' said Laurence, looking concerned. 'I FOUND IT UNDER TANGINE'S BED . . .'

CHAPTER 9

YELLOW DOESN'T SUIT YOU

'I'M SURE THERE'S A PERFECTLY GOOD EXPLANATION FOR ALL OF THIS. BUT WE NEED TO SPEAK TO TANGINE . . .' said Laurence. 'DO YOU KNOW WHERE 'E IS?'

'He went back to his pit to tidy it up,' said Amelia. 'It keeps getting mysteriously messy.'

'WELL, FIRSTLY, THERE'S BEEN NO TIDYING IN THAT PIT OF 'IS,' said Laurence. 'SECONDLY, TANGINE'S NOT THERE, SO I FORT I MIGHT FIND 'IM IN 'ERE.'

'NO, 'E'S NOT 'ERE,' said Florence.

'Maybe he went to the toilet?' suggested Grimaldi.

But nobody had time to find out because an almighty RUMBLE echoed within the pit walls. Large chunks of the ceiling began to fall to the floor, narrowly missing Amelia and her friends. '*What's happening?!*' she yelled, as she scooped Squashy up into her arms.

'GET OUT OF THE PIT!' shouted Laurence.

Grimaldi appeared frozen to the spot, bracing his scythe tightly.

Florence swiftly lifted the stunned Grimaldi up under one arm and the friends ran as fast as they could out of their pit. Then, what was once their sleeping quarters collapsed into a big pile of rubble with a loud

CRAAAAAAASH!

The friends stood in shocked silence as clouds of dust slowly rose from the debris.

'WHAT THE ACTUAL BATS?!' Florence finally blurted out.

Grimaldi awoke from his terrified trance and began to shake. 'W . . . w . . . what happened?!'

'WE ALMOST ENDED UP ON YOUR DAD'S DEATH LIST,' said Florence.

The dust made Squashy begin sneezing. Amelia hugged him to her chest. 'It's okay, Squashy. We're safe.'

'GRIEVING GOBLINS! IS EVERYONE OKAY?' said Laurence. He put a hand on his forehead in despair. 'I CAN'T BELIEVE THAT JUST 'APPENED.'

By now, most of the ancient yetis had gathered in the tunnel, wondering what all the noise was.

Laurence stood up straight and called out above the panicked chitter-chatter of the crowd.

'EVERYONE TRY NOT TO PANIC –'

But before he could finish, two unicorns burst through the main entrance to the pits. Amelia recognised them straight away.

'*Ricky? Graham?!*' she cried as the unicorns marched in, wearing long trench coats with tiny notebooks in their top pockets.

Amelia had first met Ricky and Graham when they were unicorn guards in Glitteropolis and then later as Rainbow Ranger club leaders.

'Oh, hi Amelia!' said Ricky. 'You're probably wondering why we're here, right?'

'YEAH. WHY *ARE* YOU 'ERE?' asked Florence.

'I CALLED THEM EARLIER,' said Laurence. 'TO 'ELP SOLVE THE MYSTERY OF ALL THE MISSING FINGS.'

'We're unicorn detectives now,' said Ricky. 'And we shall SOLVE your mystery!'

'We like to broaden our horizons,' said Graham.

'We're also thinking of opening a flower shop.'

'But we're still running the Rainbow Rangers and giving out hard-earned badges, don't you worry about that!' Ricky added. Then he saw the collapsed pit and gasped. 'What happened 'ere then?'

'I'M NOT ENTIRELY SURE. THE PIT JUST . . . COLLAPSED,' said Laurence. 'THESE PITS ARE MEANT TO BE THE STURDIEST AROUND. I DON'T UNDERSTAND!'

'It's a good job I recently took a Mountain Safety course then!' said Ricky, whipping out a hard hat from his trench-coat pocket.

'BUT YOU JUST SAID YOU'RE A DETECTIVE?' said Florence.

'I am . . . but I'm also a Mountain Safety Inspector. I'm a unicorn of many talents.' Ricky winked.

'He's also been desperate to wear that hat,' sighed Graham. 'I told you Ricky, yellow doesn't suit you.'

'WELL, WE REALLY NEED TO KNOW WHAT IS GOING ON ROUND 'ERE,' said Laurence. 'AS I MENTIONED TO YOU ON THE PHONE, FINGS JUST KEEP GOING MISSING. ALTHOUGH WE DID FIND MARGOT'S TIARA . . . IN TANGINE'S PIT.'

'Can we speak to the young prince?' asked Graham. 'That would be the best way to kick off our investigation.'

'WELL, THAT'S THE FING, I DON'T KNOW WHERE 'E IS,' said Laurence.

'Maybe he's HIDING!' said Margot, holding on to her tiara tightly. 'He was particularly interested in my tiara when he first saw it. Seems a bit odd that it should go missing, then turn up in his room!'

'WHAT ARE YOU SUGGESTING?' said Florence with a frown.

'I'm not suggesting anything,' said Margot. 'It just seems . . . *odd.*'

'Hey! Tangine would never take anything!' cried Amelia. 'Shouldn't we be more concerned with trying to find *him*? What if he's in trouble?'

'QUITE RIGHT!' Laurence called out, smiling at Amelia. 'LET'S NOT GET CARRIED AWAY. I'M SURE THERE'S A GOOD EXPLANATION FOR ALL OF THIS. AND THAT'S WHY THE UNICORN DETECTIVES ARE 'ERE. SO LET 'EM DO THEIR JOB AND 'OPEFULLY THEY'LL FIND TANGINE IN THE PROCESS.'

CRASH!

Yetis screamed and bellowed as another two pits collapsed at the same time.

'*What's happening?!*' cried Margot.

Suddenly, cracks appeared in the walls all around the tunnel. A long CREEEEEEEEEEEAAAAAK resonated through the mountain pits.

Then there was silence.

'Well, that didn't sound good,' said Graham.

Ricky galloped over to the crack in the wall and pulled a tape measure out from his trench coat. He measured the length of the crack and began scribbling in his notepad and muttering calculations to himself. Then he trotted forwards to study another crack in the wall, taking more measurements and scribbling more notes. Finally he paused and straightened his hard hat before returning to the group of bewildered yetis.

'I'm afraid I have some bad news,' said Ricky. 'I have only inspected a small portion of this mountain, but it's already very clear that the Yeti Mountains Pits are NOT safe.' He pointed at the cracks in the walls. 'Who knows how many more pits could collapse? These are dangerous conditions to be living in.' Ricky cleared his throat.

'Therefore, it is my duty to close these mountain pits down!'

'WHAT?!' said Laurence.

'I'm sorry,' said Ricky. 'It's too much of a risk to stay here.'

'BUT THIS 'AS BEEN THE ANCIENT YETIS' 'OME SINCE THEY RETIRED,' said Laurence. ''OW LONG DO WE 'AVE TO GET OUT?'

Ricky looked at Graham awkwardly, then back at Laurence. 'I'm afraid everyone will have to leave the Yeti Mountain Pits right now.'

CHAPTER 10

A THOUSAND MILES AWAY

A few of the ancient yetis began wailing.

'WHERE ARE ALL THE YETIS MEANT TO GO?!' said Laurence. 'THEY'RE ANCIENT. WE NEED TO FIND 'EM A NEW 'OME BEFORE SUNRISE UVVAWISE THEY WON'T 'AVE ANYWHERE TO SLEEP!'

'Ricky,' said Graham. 'Where was that massive mountain we saw when we went travelling last year?'

'Oh yeah, it was HUGE!' said Ricky. 'I think it was on that remote island about a thousand miles away. Only ghosts live there, but they're a friendly, transparent bunch.

I think it was called Ghouling Isle. Yeh, that's right. Lovely place. Bit dead though.'

'There you go!' said Graham with a big smile. 'Sounds like the perfect place to dig new pits. Plenty of room for new residents to roam on the island, and it was a MASSIVE mountain, so you could dig some proper penthouse suites!'

'And y'never know,' Ricky added. 'You might get a free haunting while you're at it.' He paused. 'You don't look happy, Laurence.'

Florence's dad was frowning hard. 'YOU'RE SUGGESTING WE MOVE A FOUSAND MILES AWAY?'

'Well, I can't think of anywhere nearer with a big enough mountain for all of you,' said Graham sadly. 'Can you?'

Laurence's expression fell. He looked at the group of yetis and let out a long sigh. 'NO,' he said. 'I CAN'T . . .'

'*Noooooooooooo!*' cried Margot. 'I don't want to leave Nocturnia!'

'Agreed!' yelled Derek. 'THIS is our home!'

Grand-yeti Clemence rushed over. 'THERE MUST BE SUMFIN' WE CAN DO, LAURENCE?'

Laurence sighed. 'YOU 'EARD THE UNICORN DETECTIVES, IT'S NOT SAFE 'ERE NO MORE.' He placed a paw gently on Clemence's shoulder. 'I CAN'T RISK YOU ALL GETTING SQUISHED IN 'ERE. SO, WE NEED TO FIND A MOUNTAIN BIG ENOUGH AND STURDY ENOUGH FOR EVERYONE TO MOVE TO. IT SOUNDS LIKE GHOULING ISLE IS OUR ONLY OPTION.'

'BUT DAD,' said Florence. 'IF THE NEW PITS ARE A FOUSAND MILES AWAY ON A REMOTE ISLAND, 'OW ARE YOU MEANT TO GET THERE EVERY NIGHT TO LOOK AFTER EVERYONE?'

Laurence stroked Florence's head affectionately. 'WE'LL 'AVE TO MOVE TO GHOULING ISLE TOO,' he said sadly.

'WHAT?' Florence started, then gulped. 'BUT I WON'T SEE MY FRIENDS IF WE MOVE THAT FAR AWAY!'

'THEY CAN COME AND VISIT,' said Laurence, giving Florence a big hug. 'NOW I MUST GET YOU ALL OUT OF 'ERE IN CASE MORE PITS COLLAPSE.'

Florence fell silent. Her dad stepped forward and spoke with deep regret.

'EVERYONE PACK YOUR FINGS AND MEET OUTSIDE THE MOUNTAIN IN THE NEXT HOUR PLEASE.'

Florence didn't say anything. Amelia felt her heart drop into her stomach and her stomach drop into her toes. *Florence had to move a THOUSAND miles away*?

Another loud groan resonated through the

mountain and a huge crack stretched across the floor. The yetis screamed and clutched each other tightly.

Then there was a huge CRAAAAAASH from further along the tunnel as more pits began to collapse, one after the other. It was as if a giant yeti was smashing its way through the walls.

CRAAAAAASH!

CRAAAAAAASH!

'EVERYONE OUTSIDE! THERE'S NO TIME TO PACK YOUR FINGS!' shouted Florence's dad. 'FLO, GET YOUR FRIENDS OUT!'

CRAAAAAAASH!

‘‘OLD ON TO YER KNICKERS!’ cried Clemence.

‘I have no knickers on!’ another yeti wept.

Squashy squeaked in alarm and Amelia hugged him tightly to her chest.

Panic scorched through Amelia’s veins like hot scream tea as the pits collapsed around them. *Tangine was still missing*.

Amelia ran up to Laurence and tugged at

his jacket sleeve. 'Mr Spudwick! Tangine's still not here!' she said urgently. 'He'll be in danger!'

Laurence gave Amelia a determined look. 'I'LL MAKE SURE WE FIND 'IM, DON'T WORRY,' he said. 'BUT YOU *MUST* GET SAFELY OUTSIDE FIRST.'

'We can't just leave him!' said Amelia, almost in tears, as Grimaldi and Florence clutched hands behind her.

'I'LL FIND 'IM, I PROMISE,' Laurence reassured her. He put a paw on each of Amelia's shoulders and looked at her with a kind but serious expression. 'I KNOW THESE PITS BETTER THAN ANYONE . . . I DUG 'EM AFTER ALL. BUT I 'AVE TO MAKE SURE EVERYONE STAYS SAFE AND THAT INCLUDES *YOU*. I'LL GO FIND TANGINE AS SOON AS YER ALL OUTSIDE. YOU JUST GOTTA TRUST ME . . . CAN YOU DO THAT?'

Amelia felt a lump in her throat, but eventually nodded.

Laurence squeezed her shoulders. 'NOW QUICKLY, OFF YOU GO!'

Once Ricky and Graham had ushered the ancient yetis out and everyone was safely huddled outside, Laurence began a final head count.

Amelia, Florence and Grimaldi watched in horror as the Yeti Mountain Pits literally began crumbling in front of them.

'WHERE'S TANGINE?!' said Florence, scanning the crowd.

'Your dad said he's going to find him,' said Amelia shakily.

'What if he's stuck under a collapsed pit?!' gasped Grimaldi.

Florence frowned and looked towards the entrance to the pits.

'I'M NOT WAITING FOR DAD,' said Florence, taking a deep breath. 'I'M GOIN' IN!' And she ran back into the pits.

Amelia held Squashy tight under one arm, then gave Grimaldi a knowing look. She knew what they had to do.

Before anyone had a chance to stop them, they rushed back into the Yeti Mountain Pits behind Florence.

'KIDS! NO!' shouted Florence's dad.

But before he could to stop them, the entrance to the pits collapsed.

And the friends were left in total darkness.

CHAPTER 11

GREAT GLITTER GATHERER

'ARGH! I CAN'T SEE A FING!' said Florence.

'Hold on . . .' said Grimaldi. With a small CLICK, his scythe began to glow.

Amelia gave Squashy a reassuring squeeze.

'Oh man, we're so totally doomed,' said Grimaldi, shining his scythe towards the completely and utterly blocked exit.

The friends were silent for a moment. Then Florence spoke.

'WELL, BETTER TO BE DOOMED TOGEVVA I GUESS.'

'I don't want you to leave Nocturnia, Florence,' Amelia said quietly. 'If I'd known this was going to happen, I'd never have tried to leave the party early.' Amelia looked down, tears welling up in her eyes. Squashy tried to lick them off her cheeks. 'I'm so sorry,' she whispered.

Amelia felt a big hairy paw fall on her shoulder.

'WELL, DON'T BE,' said Florence. When Amelia looked up, she saw that Florence was smiling.

'I'M SORRY TOO. I WAS ONLY FINKING OF MYSELF. IT'S JUST, WE USED TO DO EVERYFINK TOGEVVA AND NOW, WELL, WE'RE STARTING TO DO DIFFERENT STUFF AND OF COURSE WE'RE GONNA MAKE NEW FRIENDS . . .' Florence looked sad. 'I WAS JUST WORRIED YOU MIGHT NOT WANNA HANG OUT WIV ME AS MUCH, COZ YOUR NEW FRIENDS LOVE PUMPKINS AND ALL THAT STUFF, AND ARE PROB'LY WAY MORE INTERESTING THAN ME.'

Amelia took Florence's paw and squeezed it tight. 'Nobody is more interesting than you, Florence Spudwick,' she said with a smile.

'I'm certainly not,' Grimaldi added with a wink.

'I JUST DON'T WANT YOU TO FORGET ABOUT ME,' sniffed Florence. 'ESPECIALLY NOW I 'AVE TO MOVE REALLY FAR AWAY. I WON'T SEE YOU AS MUCH.'

Squashy *pa-doinged* out of Amelia's arms and nibbled at Florence's toes affectionately.

'There is no WAY we could forget about you,' Amelia chuckled. 'You're far too big and fluffy for that!'

Florence wrapped her arms around Amelia, and pulled Grimaldi into a big hug, then nearly slipped over backwards.

'WOAH!' said Florence, finding her balance. 'I JUST TROD IN A MASSIVE PATCH OF GLITTER . . . WHERE'D THAT COME FROM?'

Grimaldi held his scythe up to get a better look around.

'Hey, look, there's another patch over there!' he said, pointing into the tunnel. In the glow of the scythe light, small blobs of glitter twinkled all around the walls and in amongst the rubble.

'LOOKS AS IF TANGINE'S BEEN FLAPPIN' 'IS WINGS ALL OVER THE PLACE!'

said Florence with a chuckle. 'COME ON, WE'D BETTER GO FIND 'IM BEFORE WE'RE TURNED INTO PUTRID PANCAKES BY ANUVVA COLLAPSING PIT.'

'Where do we start though?' said Grimaldi. 'We have NO idea where Tangine is.'

Amelia caught sight of the notice board which was glimmering fiercely with pictures of all of the yetis' "*MISSING FINGS*".

Suddenly something occurred to her.

'Grimaldi, can you shine your scythe a little closer to these pictures please?'

'Sure,' said Grimaldi, floating to Amelia's side.

Amelia gasped.

'YOU OKAY?' said Florence.

Amelia felt like her brain was doing somersaults. 'GLITTER!' she cried.

'Um, what?' said Grimaldi, looking confused.

Amelia began pointing at the pictures and mumbling under her breath. 'Margot's tiara, Derek's bubble flute, Clemence's necklace, Jane's flamingo-dragon knickers, reading glasses, Glitteropolis socks, sparkly disco ball, unicorn earrings, ballet shoes . . .'

'I FINK SHE'S FINALLY LOST THE PLOT,' Florence whispered to Grimaldi.

'Can't you see? Everything that went missing has something in common . . .' said Amelia. 'They're ALL GLITTERY!'

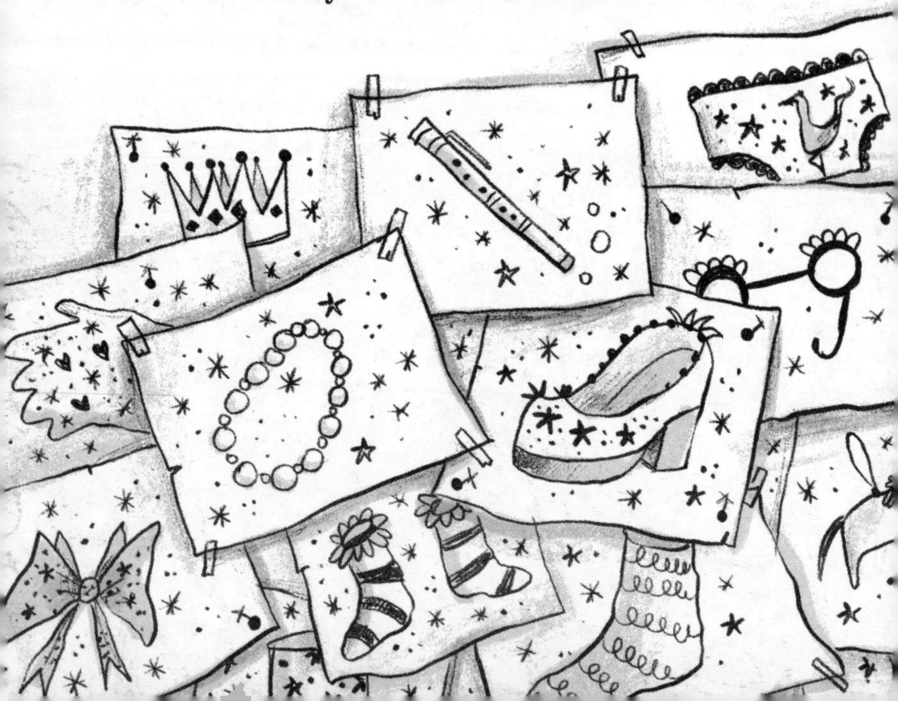

'Oooh, and Tangine's glitter polish too!' Grimaldi added. Then he gasped. 'AND TANGINE HIMSELF.'

'EXACTLY!' Amelia shrieked.

'WOW, DEEP BREATH GUYS,' said Florence. 'YOU MIGHT BURST A KIDNEY IF YOU'RE NOT CAREFUL.'

'There's a VERY glittery theme here! Think about it . . .' said Amelia, pacing back and forth. 'If something or someone HAS been taking glittery things, then *maybe* they've taken Tangine, too?'

'OOOH, THAT WOULD MAKE SENSE,' said Florence. 'GOOD FINKING, AMELIA!'

Amelia fumbled around in her cloak and pulled out the old map.

'Guys! Remember that map we were looking at earlier? Well, maybe it's all connected in some way,' she said, waving around the crinkled paper. 'I just can't help feeling it wasn't a coincidence that I found this map hidden in Tangine's room . . .'

'Maybe Tangine was set up to look like he stole the items?' suggested Grimaldi.

'Maybe,' said Amelia in deep thought.

'WHAT ARE YOU FINKING, AMELIA?' asked Florence curiously.

'I'm not entirely sure . . . If there was treasure hidden in this mountain once before,' said Amelia, 'then maybe Tangine and the yetis' missing glittery things have been taken to that place again.'

She straightened up and said with determination, 'Maybe it's time to have that adventure you wanted, Florence. Let's follow the map!'

'X marks the spot?' said Grimaldi hopefully.

Florence straightened up. 'LET'S DO IT,' she said boldly. 'LET'S GO RESCUE PRINCE LA FLOOFLE AND PROVE 'IS INNOCENCE! AND IF I 'AVE TO LEAVE NOCTURNIA, I MAY AS WELL 'AVE ONE LAST EPIC ADVENTURE WIV YOU GUYS TO REMEMBER IT BY!'

CHAPTER 12

NOPE

'SO, IT LOOKS LIKE THE BIG X IS AT THE VERY BOTTOM OF THE PITS,' said Florence, looking at the map. 'WE CAN TAKE THE YETIVATOR DOWN.'

Amelia, Florence and Grimaldi set off for the yetivator at the end of the main tunnel. Florence pressed the big red button, but the yetivator didn't move.

'OH, THAT'S NOT GOOD,' said Florence, prodding the button. 'LOOKS LIKE IT'S BROKEN. PROBABLY FROM ALL THE COLLAPSING PITS. WE'LL 'AVE TO TAKE THE LONG WAY DOWN.'

The friends made their way down rickety staircases and wove in and out of long tunnels, careful not to trip over loose rubble from the collapsed pits. Gaping holes were left in the walls where pits had once been, and the ancient yetis' belongings were scattered amongst the debris.

'How far down are we, Florence?' asked Amelia.

'WE STILL 'AVE A WAY TO GO,' said Florence. 'IT'S A *BIIIIIG* MOUNTAIN!'

'This is going to take us *forever*!' sighed Grimaldi.

'Actually . . .' said Amelia, pointing ahead, 'I think it's going to take a little longer than forever.'

A huge pile of wreckage from the remains of a collapsed pit was blocking the rest of their way.

'*What are we meant to do now?*' said Grimaldi, clutching his scythe tightly.

'There must be another way,' said Amelia, frantically studying the map.

Florence grunted. 'THERE *IS* . . .' she paused. 'BUT I DON'T FINK YOU'RE GONNA LIKE IT.'

'Why?' said Grimaldi shakily. 'What *is* it?'

'IT'S A CHUTE. LIKE A KIND OF SLIDE,' said Florence, not making eye contact.

'Well, that doesn't sound too bad?' said Amelia.

'IT'S THE RUBBISH CHUTE.'

'Oh . . .' said Amelia and Grimaldi in unison.

The friends followed the map along the dark tunnels to where Florence had indicated the rubbish chute was, with only Grimaldi's scythe to light the way.

Suddenly Amelia thought she felt something brush past her feet and squealed, which in turn caused Grimaldi to scream and jump into Florence's arms.

'WHAT'S GOING ON?!' said Florence. 'WHY ARE YOU BOTH SCREAMING LIKE GOONS?'

'Because *Amelia* screamed!' said Grimaldi, clutching Florence's fur.

'WHY DID AMELIA SCREAM?'

Amelia took a deep breath. 'I just felt something brush past my leg and it made me jump,' she said. 'Sorry . . . maybe it was just my imagination.'

Squashy began sniffing around and squeaked at something behind her.

'MAYBE IT WAS JUST SQUASHY?' suggested Florence. 'E'S ALWAYS UNDER YOUR FEET!'

Squashy waggled his stalk indignantly.

Amelia looked back. In the darkness, she swore she saw something move in the

shadows – but when she blinked, it was gone.

'OKAY, I FINK WE'RE AT THE RUBBISH CHUTE,' said Florence.

In front of them was a large, dark opening. Grimaldi shone his scythe inside to get a better look, then floated back silently.

'I ALWAYS WANTED TO SLIDE DOWN THIS AS A TODDLER, BUT DAD NEVER LET ME,' said Florence.

'Maybe because it's a chute for *rubbish*?' said Grimaldi.

'NAH, THAT WOULD NEVER PUT A YETI OFF,' Florence chuckled.

Grimaldi looked at the chute. 'Nope,' he said.

'Nope, what?' Amelia asked, confused.

'WHAT DO YOU MEAN "NOPE"?' said Florence. 'IT'S JUST A BIG SLIDE. YOU LIKE SLIDES, RIGHT?'

'Nope,' said Grimaldi, frozen to the spot.

'Is there no other way of getting to the bottom pits?' Amelia asked, feeling a little sorry for Grimaldi.

'NOPE,' said Florence.

Amelia rubbed Grimaldi's shoulder. 'You can do this! Just think of it as a big fun slide at the Ferocious Fun Fair.' She smiled and gave Grimaldi a friendly nudge.

'I hate the slides,' he said with a shaky voice. 'There's nothing *fun* about them . . .'

'COME ON GRIMALDI,' said Florence. 'THIS IS OUR ONLY WAY DOWN . . . WE 'AVE TO FIND TANGINE BEFORE THIS 'OLE PLACE COLLAPSES! AND REMEMBER, THIS IS OUR LAST ADVENTURE BEFORE I 'AVE TO LEAVE NOCTURNIA. DON'TCHA WANT ME TO REMEMBER YOU AS THE BRAVE AND MIGHTY GRIMALDI?!'

Grimaldi took a few deep breaths and composed himself. 'Okay . . . brave and mighty,' he said calmly. 'I can be brave and mighty. Except . . . um . . . What's *that*?' he said, pointing a shaky finger down the tunnel, behind Amelia and Florence.

The two friends swung round to see two green glowing eyes.

Grimaldi's eye sockets grew wider by the second. '*Aaaaaaaaaaaaaargh!* It's heading straight for us! What the bats IS it?! IT'S GOING TO ATTACK US!'

Grimaldi entered full-blown panic mode, stumbled backwards and fell head first straight into the rubbish chute.

‘*GAAAAAAAAAAAAAAAAAAAAAAAAH!*’ echoed Grimaldi’s voice as he slid away into the darkness.

Without warning, Squashy bounced into the chute behind Grimaldi.

‘WAIT SQUASHYYYYYYYYY!’ Amelia squealed, then jumped in herself.

‘ALRIGHTY THEN . . .’ said Florence, taking one last fearful look at the green eyes in the tunnel and psyching herself up. ‘GUESS IT’S MY TURN!’ And she launched herself into the chute. ‘HERE I GOOOOOOOOOOOOOOOOOOOOOOO!’

CHAPTER 13

WHY AM I INSIDE THE WALLS?

'GAAAAAAAAAAAAAAAAAAAAAAAAAAAAH!'

As Amelia slid down, Florence shot past her in the chute, but managed to grab Amelia's hand at the very last second. The two friends went whizzing together down the terrifyingly steep slope. The rush of air made it hard to see what was going on. Amelia tried to sit up straight, but they were just moving too fast.

'WE 'AVE TO CATCH UP WIV SQUASHY AND GRIMALDI!' Florence shouted breathlessly. 'BUT WE NEED TO BE MORE

STREAMLINED! COPY ME! LEGS TOGEVVA. POINT YOUR TOES. AND ARMS TIGHT BY YOUR SIDES. IT'LL MAKE YOU SLIDE FASTER!'

Amelia didn't think she could slide any quicker, but as soon as she did what Florence suggested, she felt the rush of air whizz even faster past her ears! Grimaldi's screaming began to grow louder and soon Amelia spotted the glow of his scythe down the chute ahead.

Squashy was rolling so fast by Grimaldi's side that Amelia could hardly see him. He was a little orange blur.

'*SQUAAAAAAASHY!*' she called.

'*GRIMAAAAAAALDI!*' Florence shouted as loud as she could. '*WE'RE RIGHT BEHIND YAAAAAAA!*'

But then, just as Amelia thought they were about to catch them up, both Squashy and Grimaldi disappeared – as if by magic.

Amelia and Florence shot down the chute until they flew out of its mouth into a great big pit FULL of rubbish.

Amelia took in a deep breath, then really wished she hadn't – the smell was AWFUL. She removed a mouldy eyeball stuck to her cheek.

'Are they here?!' she asked, urgently digging through all the rubbish, her heart pounding. 'SQUASHY?! GRIMALDI?! *Where are you?!*'

Florence began to panic-dig. Gooey limbs, strange broken objects and copious amounts of mouldy food went flying everywhere, bouncing off the walls of the pit as Florence's large hairy arms ploughed through the mounds of rubbish in search of their friends.

But finally, even Florence gave up. She and Amelia had to admit the obvious. Grimaldi and Squashy weren't in the rubbish pit with them.

So, where had they gone?

Florence looked around, a trail of intestine dangling from her ear and an empty tin can in her hand. 'I DON'T GET IT! THEY WERE RIGHT IN FRONT OF US. SQUASHMEISTER? GRIMALDI?!'

Amelia couldn't speak, she was so upset. They'd already lost Tangine. And now they'd lost Squashy and Grimaldi too. Florence looked at her sadly.

Then, in the silence, they heard something.

'*Guuuuuuys?*'

Florence looked at the tin can in her paw in confusion then held it up to her face.

'*GRIMALDI?!* YOU IN THERE?'

'I'm not entirely sure where I am, but Squashy's here with me and he's fine too,' echoed Grimaldi's voice. 'Well, he's kind of wedged under my belly . . . so actually he could be better.'

There was a small *squeeeeak* that made Amelia sigh with relief.

'*Where are you guys?!*' called Grimaldi.

'We're in a big bin!' Amelia answered. 'How come we can *hear* you but we can't *see* you? This is so weird!'

'I know, right?' said Grimaldi's voice. 'One minute I was sliding and screaming and the next minute I flew off to the side and got lodged inside what I THINK is a small tunnel just big enough for me. Florence *definitely* wouldn't fit in here.'

'OI!' said Florence.

'Then Squashy flew in behind me,' Grimaldi continued, 'and now I'm lodged in even further. Then, well, I heard your voices, and here we are! And you won't believe how much glitter is in here. I'm covered in it!'

'SO GRIMALDI AND SQUASHY ARE WEDGED IN A SMALL GLITTERY TUNNEL INSIDE THE WALL, AND WE'RE SITTING IN A MASSIVE BIN,' said Florence. 'THIS IS A VERY STRANGE SITUATION.'

'Ooo, I've found something,' said Grimaldi. 'It looks like a half-eaten shoe . . . It's so shiny. WAIT . . .' He went quiet for a moment. 'I recognise this shoe! I know its smell . . .'

'What do you mean?' asked Amelia. 'What does it smell like?'

'It smells like unicorn fart and . . . *magnificence,'* said Grimaldi.

'TANGINE!' said Amelia and Florence in unison.

'If Tangine's shoe is in the mystery hidden tunnel with Grimaldi, then where is

TANGINE?' Amelia pondered. 'And WHY is his shoe inside the wall?'

'More to the point, *why are we inside the wall*?' Grimaldi added. 'Did I ever mention I start to panic when I'm in small enclosed spaces?'

'YOU PANIC ABOUT EVERYFINK, SO THAT'S NO SURPRISE,' Florence replied. 'SURELY, WE MUST BE CLOSE TO TANGINE IF 'IS SHOE IS 'ERE . . .'

Amelia scratched her head, deep in thought. 'Okay, so we need to work out how to get Grimaldi and Squashy out

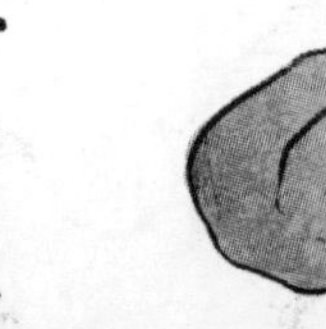

of the wall first,' she said. 'Then we can try to figure out where Tangine is . . .'

But Amelia didn't have time to work anything out, because right at that moment there was a very loud rumbling sound. And then a long crack appeared in the pit wall above Amelia and Florence's heads.

'UH OH,' said Florence.

'Why is Florence *uh-oh*ing?!' Grimaldi's small voice shrieked. '*What's going on?!*'

Everything was silent for a second, before another bigger crack opened up. Something round and orange fell from the ceiling, narrowly missing Florence's head.

'*Squashy!*' cried Amelia. She waded through a pile of cabbage and wrapped her arms around the little pumpkin.

And then Grimaldi followed with a PLOP as he fell into a big pile of gooey plug-hair.

Grimaldi gagged. 'I think I'd rather be back in the confined spaces of the walls than in here!' he said.

'GLAD TO 'AVE YOU BACK!' said Florence, putting a big arm around the little reaper.

CREEEEEEEEEEAAAAAAAAAAAAK!

‘UH-OH,’ said Florence.

‘Great, another uh-oh,’ said Grimaldi. ‘What now?!’

‘I FINK THE RUBBISH PIT MIGHT COLLAPSE AT ANY MINUTE,’ said Florence. ‘WE NEED TO GET OUT. FAST!’

But they weren’t fast enough. Another crack appeared, and this time it was the crack to end all cracks.

Chunks of pit came crashing down into the pile of rubbish. The walls crumbled. And the pit finally collapsed on top of the three friends and the little pumpkin.

CHAPTER 14

SHOUTING!

Dust settled and there was complete silence. Just debris and destruction.

Florence was scrunched over, using her body to protect her friends.

Her back had taken the brunt of the fallen rubble. Her dress was in tatters, her glasses were broken, and her fur was tangled.

'YOU ALL OKAY?' she croaked.

Amelia, who had held Squashy safely beneath her, looked up to see Florence grimacing. Her eyes were closed tight. 'I FINK IT'S SAFE NOW . . .' she said, straightening up slowly. She paused. 'OH . . .'

'Florence!' cried Amelia, crawling out from underneath her. 'Are you hurt?'

Florence finished straightening up, then raised her eyebrows.

'ME BACK'S FINE,' she finally said. 'BUT I FINK IT'S SAFE TO SAY ME KNICKERS ARE ON SHOW . . .'

She turned around and, sure enough, her dress had been completely shredded, revealing her patterned knickers.

'GOOD JOB I WORE ME BEST PAIR, EH?!' said Florence with a grin.

Amelia wasn't sure whether to laugh or cry. So, she did both.

She and Grimaldi hugged Florence tightly.

'You saved us!' Amelia choked through a sob. 'Thank you!' Squashy nuzzled into Amelia's chest and squeaked twice.

'Okay, we'd better hurry and find Tangine before the *whole* mountain collapses once and for all!' said Amelia urgently.

'Um, guys,' said Grimaldi. He was staring up above them, looking very concerned. '*Look!*'

The friends looked up and could see the glow of the moon miles above their heads. The core of the mountain had completely collapsed, creating one huge crater – and the friends were at the very bottom.

But the strangest thing of all was the magical light which glowed out from the insides of the newly exposed mountain walls.

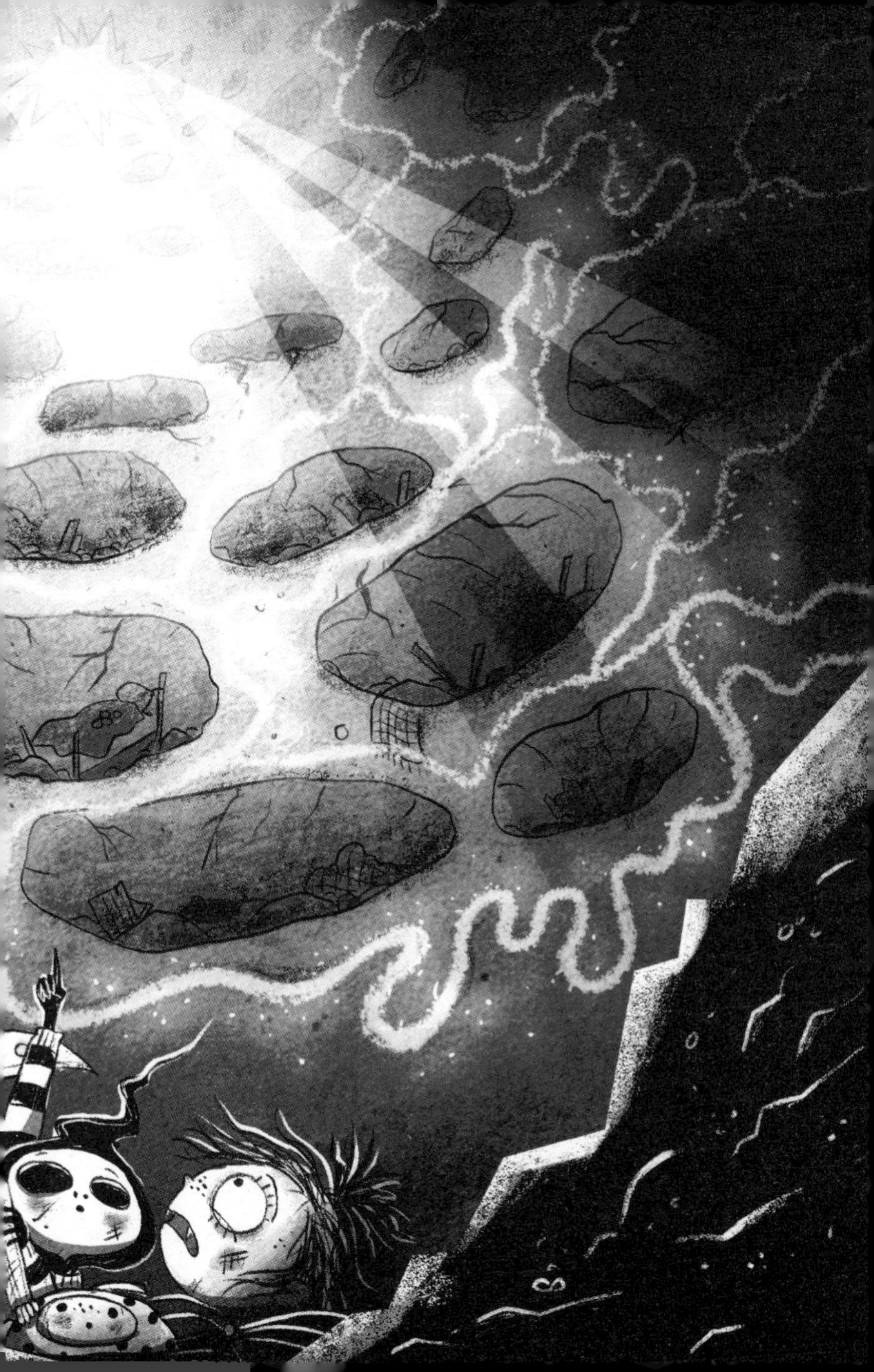

It was now clear where Grimaldi had been stuck. Hundreds of tiny tunnels wove around each other like chaotic spider webs, and they sparkled fiercely, shining a glittery light on the friends' upturned faces.

'Wow,' said Amelia. 'It's like a tiny yeti has been burrowing inside the walls of the pits!'

'And it also looks as though they've been using Tangine's glitter polish!' said Grimaldi, squinting at the glimmering trails.

The thought of Tangine's glitter polish made Amelia's heart swell. 'Oh, Tangine,' she sighed. 'I really hope he's okay.'

Amelia looked at the treasure map, which was almost in complete tatters. She just hoped that there was still enough of it to lead them to Tangine and the missing yeti treasures. Squashy kept sniffing at the map and making strange noises.

'Squashy!' said Amelia, gently placing him

on the debris. 'I need to see where the X is so you'll have to stop sniffing around it for a moment.'

Then Amelia gasped. 'Wait a minute . . . it looks like the X is right underneath us,' she said.

'WELL THAT CAN'T BE RIGHT. THERE'S NUFFIN' UNDERNEATH THE RUBBISH PIT,' said Florence. 'WE'RE AS FAR DOWN AS THE PITS GO.'

She took the map from Amelia and grunted. 'HMMM, YOU ARE RIGHT THOUGH . . . I'M BAFFLED.'

'We'll never find Tangine now!' said Amelia, feeling hopeless. 'All the X leads us to is a big pile of rubbish – with a mountain full of rubble on top!'

'And to make matters worse, I can't see any way out of here,' said Grimaldi, holding his glowing scythe up to get a good look around.

'The tunnels are far too small for Florence to climb through and all the original big yeti ones have collapsed!'

Suddenly, with a triumphant squeak, Squashy pa-doinged through a gap in the rubble into the rubbish below and completely disappeared.

'Squashy!' yelled Amelia. 'Hey! Come back! What are you doing?!' She reached into the rubble where Squashy had disappeared, but instead of finding the little pumpkin, her hands went straight through a very mouldy brain-pie.

Ignoring the ripe smell of long-forgotten food waste, Amelia rummaged around, flinging half-eaten scab-cakes, dregs of wilted spinach and the odd limb; a big toe narrowly missed hitting Florence in the face.

'HEY, HEY, CALM DOWN,' Florence said, placing a paw on Amelia's shoulder.

'We've already lost Tangine. I'm not losing Squashy too!' cried Amelia in a panic.

'I'LL GO GET SQUASHY . . .' said Florence. 'WHAT DO YETIS DO BEST?' She flexed her bicep. 'WE DIG. LOOK OUT!'

Like some kind of super-yeti, Florence threw aside great mounds of rubble until she reached the rubbish pit below. She then ploughed down with great speed through the smelly mulch until she revealed a grubby Squashy at the very bottom.

He looked up at Florence, Amelia and Grimaldi and waggled his stalk from side to side.

'Is that . . . a trap door?!' said Grimaldi, pointing towards where Squashy was sitting.

'I FINK IT IS!' said Florence. 'GOOD WORK, SQUASHMEISTER!'

Amelia clambered down to the little pumpkin and hugged him tight. 'Oh, Squashy, I'm so relieved you're okay!' She looked at the trap door. 'Do you think this is where Tangine and the treasures could be?'

'THERE'S ONLY ONE WAY TO FIND OUT!' said Florence.

She grabbed the big round handle on the trap door and pulled, but it didn't budge.

'IT'S STUCK!' she said, before yanking at the handle again.

Florence clenched her paws, drew back and punched the trap door with all her might. But it still didn't open.

'BURSTING BLISTERS!' Florence yelled, rubbing her sore knuckles. 'NEVVA IN MY LIFE 'AVE I NOT BEEN ABLE TO SMASH DOWN SUMFIN' WHEN I'VE NEEDED TO.' She frowned, raising a furry fist again. 'I REFUSE TO BE OUTDONE BY A DOOR!'

'Wait!' said Amelia suddenly. 'If it did originally lead to an ancient glittery stash, I can't imagine the door would just open easily. Maybe we need a password or something?'

'HMMM, YOU COULD BE RIGHT,' said Florence. 'BUT HOW ARE WE GONNA GUESS WHAT THE PASSWORD IS?'

'Oooh, maybe it's something yeti-related?' Amelia suggested.

'Prance!' said Grimaldi loudly. 'Fluff!' He looked excited. 'Hugs!'

Florence pulled on the door, but it didn't open. 'IT'S NOT WORKING,' she said.

'*Shouting!*' said Grimaldi.

'OI,' Florence replied.

Amelia stared intently at the door.

'STARING AT IT WON'T WORK EITHER,' said Florence after a few minutes of silence. 'IT'S NO GOOD. WE'VE LOST TANGINE, THE PITS ARE GONNA COLLAPSE AND I'LL 'AVE TO MOVE AWAY. THAT'S IF WE'RE NOT SQUISHED BY THE MOUNTAIN FIRST.'

She slumped down, plonking her big, furry bottom on to the trap door.

CLUNK!

The trap door opened right up, and Florence disappeared through it bum-first.

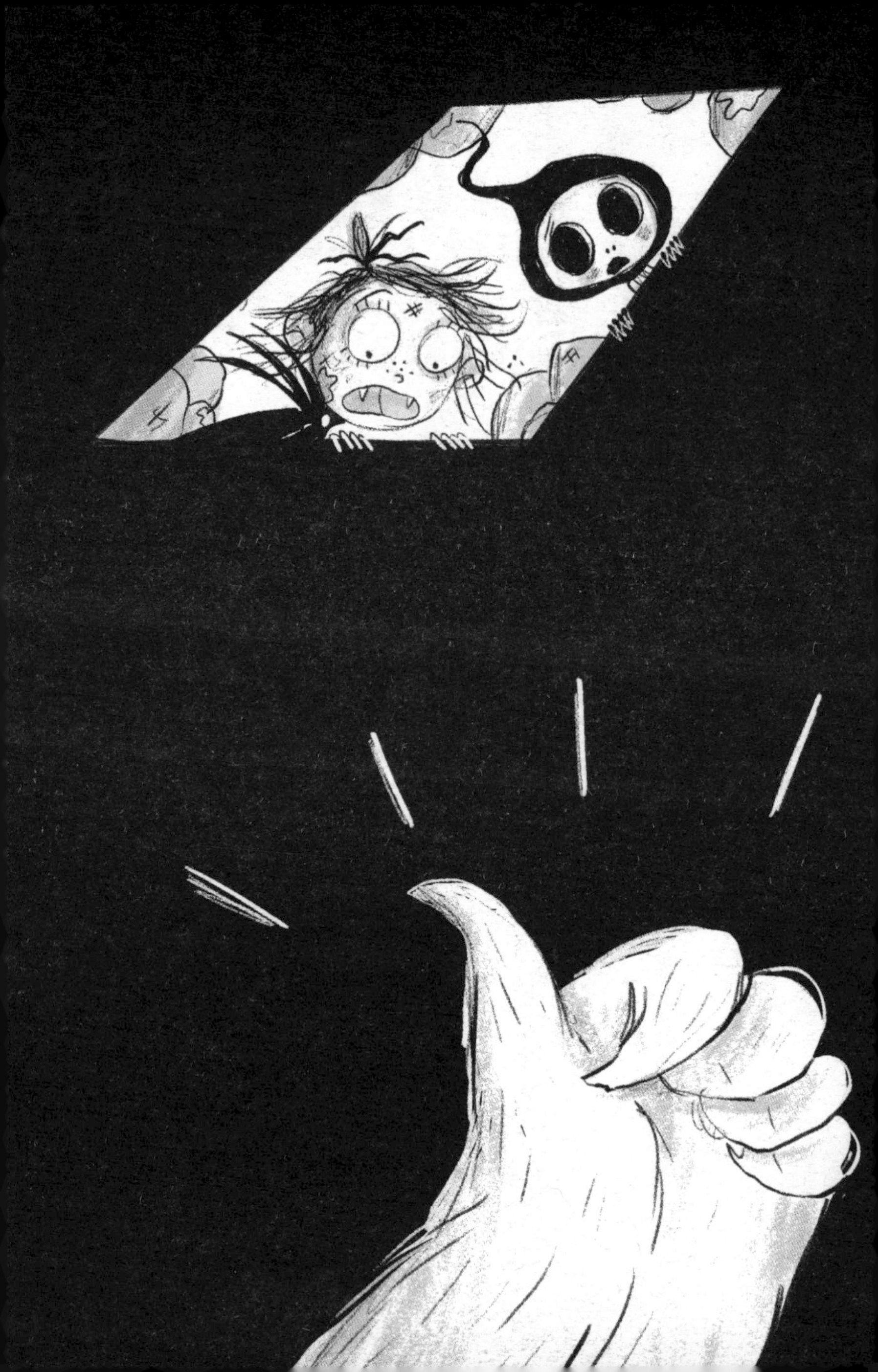

CHAPTER 15

THEY'VE SQUIDGED OUT SOME OF MY HANDSOME

'FLORENCE!' yelled Amelia and Grimaldi in unison. 'Are you okay?!'

'ALL GOOD!' Florence's voice echoed. 'I FINK A BUM-BUMP WAS THE KEY! CAN'T BELIEVE I DIDN'T FINK OF THAT!'

Squashy squeaked and pa-doinged straight through the trap door. Amelia and Grimaldi followed, landing with a PLONK.

Amelia looked round. They seemed to be in

a secret pit. A pit that was covered in shelves and dark green bottles. Underneath their bottoms, they were perched on top of a big and uncomfortable glittery pile.

'Wait a minute.' Grimaldi shone his scythe over the pile and Amelia gasped. It was all of the yetis' missing treasures! With quite a few bites taken out here and there. Amelia recognised Derek's bubble flute, Jane's flamingo-dragon knickers and Clemence's Glitteropolis Garnet necklace, amongst many other missing things from the pits.

And best of all, there in the middle of the secret pit was a very dishevelled looking . . .

'TANGINE!' Amelia, Florence and Grimaldi all cried out.

'Finally!' cried Tangine, clambering towards his friends through shimmering objects.

He was covered in dirt, his hair looked as though he'd been electrocuted, and he was missing a shoe.

'I 'AVE NEVER BEEN SO 'APPY TO SMELL UNICORN FART AND MAGNIFICENCE!' said Florence, scooping Tangine up into a big hug.

'Speaking of SMELLING, you guys smell *horrendous*. Where have you *been*?!' asked Tangine.

'In the rubbish pit,' said Grimaldi. 'That's after I was stuck in a tiny tunnel in the wall.'

'I'm not even going to ask what you were doing in the bin,' said Tangine, turning his nose up at Grimaldi.

Then he raised his eyebrows. 'Did you say you were in a tiny tunnel in the wall?'

'Yup,' said Grimaldi. 'I think I found half your shoe in there too.'

'Forget the shoe. It's a wonder I didn't lose half a limb! I've been dragged and squidged and squeezed through that tunnel more than once you know,' said Tangine, folding his arms. 'I was stuck in that same tunnel when you couldn't find me, Amelia. It leads back to the hole in the wall under my bed! But I've since realised WHAT made that tunnel . . .'

'What do you mean?' Amelia asked, looking concerned. 'Who did it, Tangine? *Who* keeps trying to kidnap you? Is it the same creature who took all the yetis' glittery treasures?!'

'You need to see it to believe it,' said Tangine, waggling his eyebrows. He pointed

upwards.
Amelia looked up and gasped. One by one, pairs of tiny green eyes appeared and multiplied in the dark cracks and crevices of the pit. Squashy began squeaking and trying to bounce up the walls.

'Come out and show yourselves, you little pests!' Tangine called out.

Slowly, one by one, out rolled lots and lots of fluffy white balls with wide toothy mouths and bright glowing eyes.

One of the strange creatures rolled all the way down into the stash of glittery items and began frantically licking at a pair of glasses. Another rolled on to Tangine's head and began nibbling at his hair.

'THESE are your culprits,' Tangine said, rolling his eyes.

Squashy was VERY excited and began bouncing around squeaking at every one of the strange creatures.

'What the bats . . .?' Amelia breathed.

'ARE THEY . . .?' Florence began.

Grimaldi cautiously approached one of the creatures to get a closer look. 'They look like . . . *fluffy* pumpkins.'

'Whatever they are, they're incredibly annoying!' said Tangine. 'When we all went back to our pits after the meeting, a load of them popped out from under my bed. When they saw me, they went positively *loopy*. They started licking my wings and it tickled so much that I fell over, and they carried me right off through the hole in the wall under my bed all the way to THIS PLACE!' He spread his arms out. 'I'm pretty sure they've squidged out some of my handsome, dragging me through the tiny tunnel.' Tangine patted his face. 'I FEEL less handsome. Do I *look* less handsome to you?'

'IT'S 'ARD TO TELL IN THIS LIGHT,' Florence replied.

Tangine scowled and shooed one of the strange pumpkins away. 'Awful little things,' he muttered grumpily.

'PUMPKINS!' said Amelia, pacing back and forth. Her mind was whirring. 'It's all making sense now!'

'I'M GLAD IT DOES TO YOU, COZ IT MAKES NO SENSE TO ME,' said Florence.

'Did you listen to ANYTHING I just said?' moaned Tangine. 'My wellbeing is AT RISK right now. I could really do with some of my

EveryKing Sparkles polish. My cheeks are horrendously dry, and it doesn't help when these ridiculous little pests keep licking and nibbling at me!'

'That's IT!' said Amelia, picking up one of the fluffy pumpkins.

She opened its mouth gently and noticed that it was FULL of glitter. She leaned in a little closer, and got a whiff of the fluffy pumpkin's breath.

'*Unicorn fart and magnificence* . . .' muttered Amelia. She placed the creature down carefully.

'Tangine, I think you'll find that

these wild pumpkins are responsible for eating your EveryKing Sparkles polish. And then, soon after your glitter polish went missing, everyone's glittery items began to disappear. Think about it . . .' Amelia continued. 'They must have got a taste for glitter and become addicted.'

Tangine gasped. 'And they must have been the ones trashing my room trying to find more!'

'MY QUESTION IS, WHERE 'AVE ALL THE FLUFFY PUMPKINS COME FROM IN THE FIRST PLACE?' said Florence.

Amelia felt like she was going to explode as all the puzzle pieces fell into place. 'I think I know EXACTLY where they've come from! And your Grand-yeti Clemence plays a part in all of this!'

'REALLY?' said Florence, looking even more confused.

'Grand-yeti Clemence told me all about the pumpkin seeds she'd planted a few months ago,' said Amelia slowly.

'ERR, YEAH,' said Florence. 'BUT NUFFIN' GREW.'

'Nothing grew that she could SEE,' said Amelia. 'When it's too cold, like it is here in the yeti mountains, pumpkins burrow down for warmth.'

'HEY! IT'S NOT TOO COLD HERE!' said Florence, miffed.

'Not if you're covered in thick furry hair, Florence,' Grimaldi said with a grin.

'Exactly, Grimaldi!' Amelia exclaimed. 'Look . . .' She rubbed at the pumpkin's soft furry belly, making it purr. 'They have thick white fur to keep warm – just like a yeti! And not only that; they have huge teeth for burrowing and glowing green eyes to see in the dark. It all makes *perfect* sense.'

‘BURROWING!’ said Florence suddenly. ‘THE FLUFFY PUMPKIN FINGS HAVE BEEN BURROWING. THAT’S WHAT CAUSED ALL THE TINY GLITTERY TUNNELS IN THE WALLS!’

‘I think they’ve been using the hole under my bed as their way in and out of the walls,’ said Tangine.

‘I guess that also explains why Florence’s dad found Margot’s tiara in your pit,’ said Amelia. ‘One of the fluffy pumpkins must have dropped it on their travels.'

'Oh man, I bet everyone thought I was the thief!' said Tangine, putting his head in his hands.

'DON'T WORRY, THEY'LL FINK DIFFERENTLY WHEN THEY SEE THESE WEIRD LITTLE GUYS . . .' said Florence.

'*We* never doubted you,' said Amelia with a smile.

'Thanks Amelia,' said Tangine.

'We thought something was strange after I found an old treasure map behind a picture frame in your room,' said Amelia. 'But it doesn't look like there *was* ever any real treasure in here. Before the wild pumpkins brought in the yetis' glittery things, of course.'

'So why would someone hide an old map leading to this place?' said Grimaldi. 'There's just a load of bottles – not one bit of treasure to be seen.'

'OH, I DUNNO ABOUT THAT,' said Florence, looking closely at the shelves on the pit walls. 'I FINK THE "TREASURE" IS ALL AROUND US . . .'

E SPUDWICK
VINTAGE
VINTAGE

CHAPTER 16

A VERY WEIRD AND STICKY SITUATION

The pit was filled with bottle upon bottle of bright green, bubbling liquid. Florence pointed at the label on one of the bottles. It read:

TERRENCE SPUDWICK'S VINTAGE SUPER-BELCH

'Wait a minute,' said Amelia. 'Didn't your Grand-yeti Clemence say Terrence was her dad?! We were drinking some of his super-belch at the party!'

'I thought Clemence said the few bottles she had were all that was left?' said Grimaldi.

'CLEARLY NOT!' said Florence, studying the old map, then looking at the bottles. '*THIS* . . .' she prodded the map – 'MUST BE GREAT GREAT GRAND-YETI TERRENCE'S MAP! 'E MUST'VE DUG A SECRET PIT TO STASH 'IS VINTAGE SUPER-BELCH, THEN MADE THIS MAP SO 'E'D REMEMBER WHERE IT WAS!'

'The pit I was staying in was Terrence's old room, so that would make sense!' Tangine added.

'I bet your Grand-yeti Clemence will be VERY glad to know there's more of this stuff!' Amelia giggled, picking up one of the bottles of super-belch.

'That's if we ever get see Clemence again!' said Grimaldi. 'We're kind of stuck down here at the moment.'

'GRIMALDI'S NOT OVER-WORRYING FOR ONCE,' said Florence. 'WE *ARE* KINDA STUCK. WITH 'UNDREDS OF BOTTLES OF BELCH AND A LOAD OF WILD PUMPKINS. A VERY WEIRD AND STICKY SITUATION INDEED.'

'Well, we need to find a way to get ourselves AND the wild pumpkins out of here safely,' said Amelia.

'But there's no way out!' said Grimaldi, hugging his scythe. 'There's no yetivator, no stairs, not even a slide we can crawl back up . . . because EVERYTHING is a pile of rubble! There's just one HUGE hole in the middle of the mountain which is WAY too high for even me to float through!'

'And my delicate fairy wings can't fly that high in this cold climate,' said Tangine sadly. 'Wait a minute, Grimaldi . . . you said *float*!'

''E JUST SAID 'E *CAN'T* FLOAT, TANGINE,' said Florence. 'NOW SHUSH. WE'RE TRYING TO FINK OF A PLAN TO GET US OUT.'

'No, I mean, the vintage super-belch will help us float!' said Tangine, picking up a bottle and opening the lid. He guzzled down a few mouthfuls and began to rise up from the ground. 'THIS, my friends, is our way out.'

Florence let out a joyous fart. 'OH, MY GLOBULE! TANGINE, YOU GENIUS!'

'This stuff is SUPER strong, right?!' Tangine continued. 'So, if we drank the WHOLE lot, that should give us enough float to get—'

'*ALL the way to the top of*

the mountain!' Amelia finished in excitement.

'Exactly!' said Tangine. He kicked out a foot a bit too enthusiastically and got a toe stuck in Florence's ear.

'Little did your great great Grand-yeti Terrence know his secret recipe would save a bunch of best friends one night,' said Amelia with a big smile. 'Hopefully your Grand-yeti Clemence won't be too upset that the very last of the secret super-belch will be gone forever?!'

Florence grunted. 'SHE DON'T 'AVE TO KNOW WE EVVA FOUND IT,' she said with a wink. 'I LIKE TO FINK THAT MAYBE ONLY *WE* WERE MEANT TO FIND IT. IT WAS ONCE TERRENCE'S LITTLE SECRET, AND NOW IT CAN BE OURS. EVEN WHEN I'M A FOUSAND MILES AWAY.'

'What do you mean, *when you're a thousand miles away*?' asked Tangine, frowning.

Amelia, Florence and Grimaldi looked at each other awkwardly.

'WELL, THE ANCIENT YETIS 'AVE TO MOVE TO A NEW MOUNTAIN A FOUSAND MILES AWAY, WHICH MEANS DAD 'AS TO MOVE TOO, AND YEAH, THAT MEANS ME AS WELL,' said Florence sadly.

Tangine looked horrified. Then he ran into Florence's furry arms and hugged her tightly. 'I'm going to fly over on John the Vulture *whenever* I can,' said Tangine. 'I'm going to miss you even more than my EveryKing Sparkles polish . . . and that's a lot.'

Amelia, Squashy and Grimaldi all joined in the big hug and tried to keep breathing as Florence squeezed them back with tears in her eyes.

She gave a big sniff and wiped her snotty nose with a big paw. 'RIGHT. WE CAN'T FINK ABOUT THAT RIGHT NOW. WE 'AVE

TO GET OUT OF 'ERE FIRST.' Florence picked up a bottle of vintage super-belch. 'LET'S DRINK UP!'

'What about all the yetis' glittery belongings?' said Grimaldi, looking at the once lost items scattered around them. 'It's going to be tricky trying to carry them all.'

Tangine picked up five pairs of glasses. 'Maybe we don't have to *carry* them all.' He put all five pairs on his face at once. 'We can *wear* them!'

Tangine was very quick to throw on a pair of platform glitter shoes, along with at least ten sparkly bracelets. Amelia wore a pair of unicorn earrings, tucked Derek's bubble flute behind her ear and put on a bunch of other strange shiny garments, whilst Grimaldi tucked a glittery disco ball in his hood and wore a collection of jewelled belts. Florence sported Jane's flamingo-dragon knickers and wore her Grand-yeti's Glitteropolis Garnet necklace.

Florence poured a few bottles of super-belch on to the floor for Squashy and the fluffy pumpkins to lap up, then the friends began to drink the rest.

Soon enough, a very bejewelled and glittering Amelia, Florence, Grimaldi and Tangine bobbed up and down in the air along with Squashy and a cluster of fluffy pumpkins, like a cloud of VERY strange balloons. They floated out of the trap door, back up through the rubbish pit and into the huge cavity in the middle of the mountain.

Amelia looked up into the moonlight and grinned.

'Okay everyone, let's FLOAT!'

Amelia led the way as the friends and the pumpkins floated up and up and up until they reached the very top of the mountain, where they were met with a rush of cold night air.

Amelia floated out first.

POP

Then Florence, Grimaldi and Tangine.

POP

POP

POP

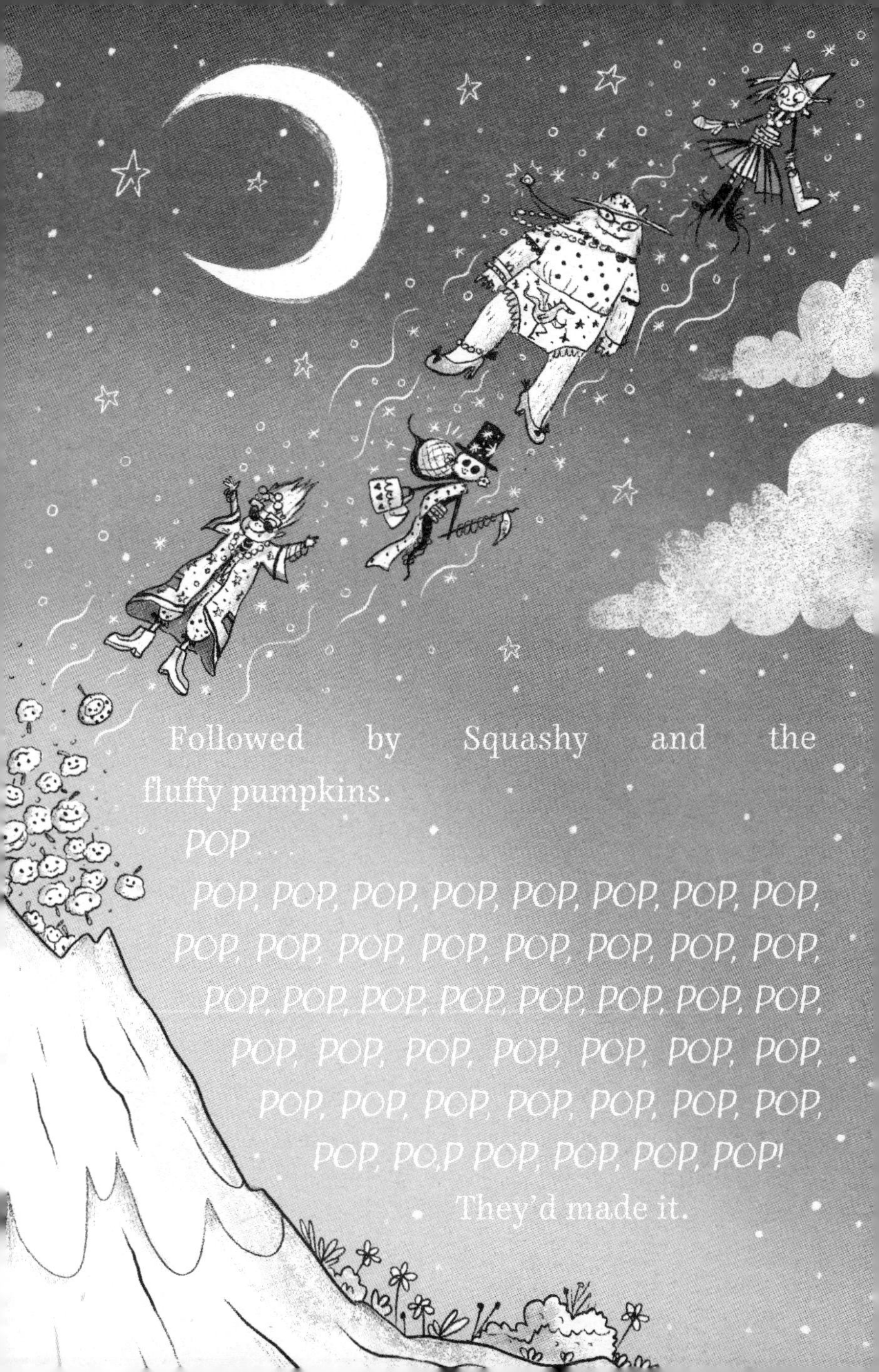

Followed by Squashy and the fluffy pumpkins.

POP . . .

POP, POP, POP, POP, POP, POP, POP, POP,
POP, POP, POP, POP, POP, POP, POP, POP,
POP, POP, POP, POP, POP, POP, POP, POP,
POP, POP, POP, POP, POP, POP, POP,
POP, POP, POP, POP, POP, POP, POP,
POP, PO,P POP, POP, POP, POP!

They'd made it.

BURP!

CHAPTER 17
FOREVER

'FLO FLO!' shouted Florence's dad, Laurence, from one side of the Yeti Mountain.

The ancient yetis began waving and cheering as Amelia and her friends floated above them in the night sky. But soon the yetis' expressions turned to confusion.

'Are they *flying*?' bellowed Derek.

'We need to float down!' Amelia called to Florence, who was directly below her.

'WE GOTTA BELCH!' said Florence. She made an almighty burping sound and began to descend slowly. Amelia, Grimaldi and Tangine followed suit, burping as loudly as they could to bring themselves back down to solid ground.

Squashy was making little burps and then squeaking at the fluffy pumpkins to do the same. They imitated Squashy with little belches and a few little farts.

'Good work, Squashy!' called Amelia.

BUUUUUUURP
BURRRRRRP
BUUUUUUUURRRRRRP

Finally, the friends landed on the side of the mountain one by one. They were greeted by a horde of emotional yetis and a very puzzled Ricky and Graham.

'OH FLO FLO! WE WERE SO WORRIED ABOUT YOU!' bellowed Laurence, running over and squeezing Florence tight in his arms. 'I'M NOT EVEN GONNA ASK WHY YOU WERE

FLOATING, OR 'OW YOU GOT OUT, OR WHY YOU'RE SURROUNDED BY STRANGE FLUFFY BALLS WIV EYES. I'M JUST SO 'APPY YOU'RE SAFE!'

Clemence ran over and hugged Amelia, Grimaldi and Tangine. 'WE FORT YOU WERE ALL GONE FOREVVA!' She sniffed. 'I'M SO RELIEVED YOU'RE ALWITE!'

'Those fluffy balls are the reason all your glittery things went missing,' said Tangine, pointing to the wild pumpkins. 'They ate my EveryKing Sparkles polish and got addicted to glitter. Then they stole all of your glittery things.' He spread out his wings and twirled around, creating his own sparkly cloud. 'Mystery solved!' he sang. The fluffy pumpkins scurried towards Tangine, eager to lap up the flecks of glitter settling to the ground.

'I FINK WE MIGHT NEED TO KEEP 'EM AWAY FROM GLITTER FOR A WHILE 'TIL THE GLITTER EFFECTS OF THE POLISH WEAR OFF!' said Florence.

'WHAT *ARE* THESE CREATURES?' asked Clemence.

'They're wild pumpkins,' said Amelia. 'I think your pumpkin seeds *did* grow . . . just not in the way you expected. You now have a WHOLE BUNCH of fluffy mountain-pumpkin pets.'

Grand-yeti Clemence gasped. 'GIDDY GOBLIN SLIME! *MY BIRFNIGHT WISH CAME TRUE!'*

'They've adapted to life in the mountains,' said Amelia. 'But they've been burrowing hundreds of tiny tunnels over the past few months whilst they've been living there to stay warm – and they've grown thick yeti fur!'

'BILLOWING BAT WINGS,' said Florence's dad. 'IT'S NO WONDER THE YETI PITS 'AVE BEEN COLLAPSING! ALL OF THOSE TINY TUNNELS IN THE MOUNTAIN WILL 'AVE BEEN WEAKENING ITS STRUCTURE.' He gasped. 'FLO FLO! WE CAN *FIX* THIS. THE TINY TUNNELS JUST NEED TO BE RE-FILLED AND THE COLLAPSED PITS CAN BE REPAIRED!'

'EVEN THOUGH THE MOUNTAIN 'AS A GAPING GREAT 'OLE IN IT?' said Florence.

'WE DIDN'T KNOW WHAT WAS CAUSING IT BEFORE, BUT NOW YOU'VE REMOVED THE ROOT OF THE PROBLEM . . .' He nodded towards the pumpkins. 'WE CAN REPAIR THE MOUNTAIN AND NO MORE PITS WILL COLLAPSE!'

Laurence put an arm around his daughter.

'NOBODY WILL BE MOVING AWAY,' he said happily. 'I RECKON ME AND YOU TOGEVVA WIV A FEW OF OUR GOOD FRIENDS CAN GET THIS PLACE UP AND RUNNING IN NO TIME! COZ AFTER ALL, WHAT DO US YETIS DO BEST, EH?'

Florence looked as though she might burst with joy.

'WE DIG!' they both bellowed, throwing their arms around each other.

Amelia felt her heart swell. 'I'm SO happy you don't have to move away, Florence!' she cried, and joined in the big furry hug.

'BUT WHERE ARE WE GONNA GO WHILST THE MOUNTAIN IS BEING FIXED?' asked Clemence.

'How about Nocturnia Palace?' suggested Tangine. 'There are over three thousand rooms and loads of Mummy Maids to help take care of you whilst Florence's dad mends the Yeti Mountain!'

'WILL THERE BE ROOM FOR ALL THE FLUFFY PUMPKINS TOO?' said Clemence, cuddling five of them at once.

'Of course!' said Tangine. 'Enough for their very own room each!'

The ancient yetis cheered and clapped and bumped bums in glee.

'So, this mystery 'as been solved by the sounds of it,' said Graham, adjusting his glasses as the unicorn and his friend emerged from the crowd.

'Easiest mystery we've ever had to solve,

Graham,' said Ricky.

'It's the *only* mystery we've ever 'ad to solve,' said Graham.

'*You* didn't even solve it!' Tangine added flatly.

'Maybe we could 'elp you rebuild your pits!' said Ricky.

'THAT WOULD BE GREAT!' said Laurence, 'WE NEED ALL THE 'ELP WE CAN GET.'

'Excellent! I've always wanted to be a yeti!' said Graham. 'Finally, my 'opes and dreams come true!'

'You can't be a yeti,' said Ricky.

'Why not?' said Graham, looking defeated.

'Coz you're a unicorn, you big orange peel,' said Ricky.

'Well, who's to say we can't ALL embrace our inner yetis and have these pits rebuilt in no time!' said Amelia with a grin. She puffed out her chest and tried flexing her arms.

'RAAAAAAAAAAAAR!' she roared.

There was silence, then everyone burst out laughing.

'OH AMELIA, YOU ARE THE FINEST YETI I'VE EVER MET,' chuckled Florence.

Over the next few weeks of the Winter Holidays, whilst the Yeti Mountain Pits were being repaired, the ancient yetis very much enjoyed their temporary stay at Nocturnia Palace.

Tangine's dad, King Vladimir, loved teaching them how to play Eye Bowls, whilst Queen Fairyweather shared books on pumpkinology with Clemence. In turn, the yetis taught the Mummy Maids how to prance, and Tangine even set up an annual Prancing Parade at the palace.

The fluffy pumpkins were also having lots of fun with Pumpy and Squashy exploring the palace gardens. Thankfully their glitter craving had worn off after about a week of a strict non-glitter diet, although their thick fur remained.

The Pumpkineers Club was going really well; Amelia even brought Florence and

Grimaldi along to a pumpkin patch race. Florence made new friends with another yeti and Grimaldi became acquainted with a pumpkin-obsessed toad. When they weren't playing together, or hanging out with new friends, Amelia, Florence and Grimaldi helped Laurence and a team of expert yeti diggers to repair the pits.

The Winter Holidays were coming to an end, and the Yeti Mountain Pits were almost as good as new. A network of smaller pits and tunnels had been specially constructed for the Yeti's new wild pumpkins to roll around if they wished.

'Y'KNOW WHAT,' said Florence as the friends sat in Central Nocturnia Graveyard eating Sugarplum ice-screams. 'I FINK

THIS IS ONE OF THE BEST WINTER 'OLIDAYS I'VE 'AD. AND I'M SO GLAD I DON'T 'AVE TO MOVE A FOUSAND MILES AWAY.'

'That's the BEST part of it all,' said Amelia. 'Even better than finding a whole bunch of wild fluffy pumpkins! And you know how much I love pumpkins . . .' She winked at Florence.

'Hey, we should give these wild pumpkins a special name,' said Grimaldi. 'Like "Fluffy Pumpkins" but much better. I'm not very good at thinking of good names though.'

'How about *tangines*!' suggested Tangine.

'NO, TANGINE,' said Florence, rolling her eyes.

'Well, they're super fluffy . . .' said Amelia, laughing. 'So, how about fluffikins?' She thought for a moment then shook her head. 'Or maybe . . . yetikins? Hmmmm, no. That still doesn't sound quite right . . .' Then she grinned. *'I've got it!'*

'WOT IS IT? TELL US!' urged Florence excitedly.

'Let's call them . . . YUMPKINS!'

'That's the perfect name!' said Tangine.

'And this is the *perfect* moment,' said Amelia, as she watched a group of fluffy yumpkins roll over the murky hills of Nocturnia and into the light of the full moon.

AMELIA FANG

Join the little
vampire with a big heart
for some howlingly hilarious adventures!

Sink your fangs into the new
AMELIA FANG
adventure
AMELIA FANG
and the
NAUGHTY CATICORNS
LAURA ELLEN ANDERSON
Coming soon!

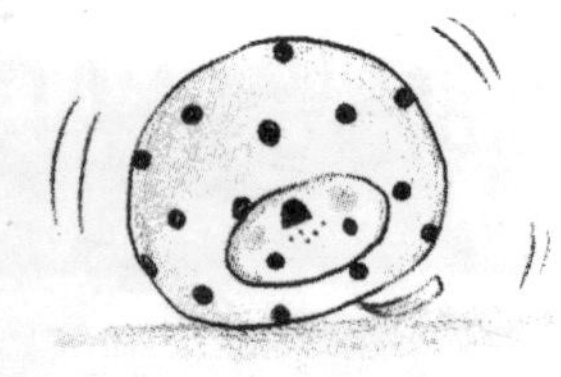

PUMPKIN
PLANS